Suddenly, Laine viewed Pat's visit with Jeff and Becca a few days earlier differently. If Pat had come to see Becca, why had she parked at Jeff's? When Becca had run to kiss the woman good-bye, Laine recalled distinctly that Pat's car had been in front of Jeff's condo, not hers. Laine's heart hammered.

So what did it mean? Were they working together? Partners in some kind of con game? Lately she'd become suspicious of everything. She couldn't believe they were the people who'd broken into her condo looking for Kathleen's jewelry or money that Laine wasn't even sure existed. She'd felt uneasy around Pat from the first day when she'd showed up unannounced at her house. She'd never understood why, but that's how she felt.

Yet she hadn't suspected Jeff. He was different. He'd been helpful. He'd even told her his friend would check on Pat. Was that only a cover-up? Laine closed her eyes, feeling betrayed and forsaken. She didn't know where to turn.

Jeff had spoken of God and forgiveness. Was it all a lie? Was his affection for her a lie? Was she another Kathleen, blindly trusting a man because she needed a friend? Needed someone to love? Her mind swirled like a raging river, and she was caught in the swift, surging current.

GAIL GAYMER MARTIN lives with her real-life hero and husband, Bob, in Lathrup Village, Michigan. Once a high-school English and public-speaking teacher, later a guidance counselor, Gail retired and taught English and speech at Davenport University. Now she is a full-time, award-winning, multipublished writer of romance fiction and the author of sixteen church resource books. Her first romance novel was published by Barbour in 1998, and in three years, God has blessed her with nearly twenty novel and novella sales.

HEARTSONG PRESENTS

Books by Gail Gaymer Martin
HP302—Seasons
HP330—Dreaming of Castles

Secrets
Within

Gail Gaymer Martin

Heartsong Presents

With love to my mom, Nellie Riley, who purchased Nancy Drew mysteries for me when I was a little girl and listened to my childhood suspense-story attempts. I am grateful for her constant guidance. She taught me to love fiction and to love my Savior above all else.

A note from the author:
I love to hear from my readers! You may correspond with me by writing:

Gail Gaymer Martin
Author Relations
PO Box 719
Uhrichsville, OH 44683

ISBN 1-58660-480-5

SECRETS WITHIN

All Scripture quotations, unless otherwise indicated, are taken from the HOLY BIBLE, NEW INTERNATIONAL VERSION®. NIV®. Copyright © 1973, 1978, 1984 by International Bible Society. Used by permission of Zondervan Publishing House. All rights reserved.

All of the characters and events in this book are fictitious. Any resemblance to actual persons, living or dead, or to actual events is purely coincidental.

Cover illustration by Jocelyne Bouchard.

PRINTED IN THE U.S.A.

one

Laine Sibley closed her eyes and drew in a ragged breath as she pressed her ear to the telephone. As her sister's voice came in tired, hesitant gasps, tears pressed against the back of Laine's eyes.

"You're okay, then, Kathleen?" Laine asked, controlling her quaking voice.

"Mavis is here. Don't worry."

Laine closed her eyes, thanking God for Mavis Dexter. The woman had become Kathleen's second mother, tending her and Becca with untiring hands. Laine couldn't imagine what it would be like to give that much time and concern for someone else. Looking up, she stared through the window and focused on Moon Lake's sun-speckled ripples a few yards from her front door. "Kiss Becca for me, and I'll see you both later."

Laine sat suspended for a moment, then pulled the phone from her ear as an afterthought and placed it on its base. Her sister's illness seemed more than she could bear.

Laine's thoughts filled with images of Kathleen's five-year-old daughter, Rebecca. With her dark waving hair and ivory skin, the child was the image of her Irish father, who had been killed in a plane crash. Picturing Becca's sad blue eyes, Laine ached for the child and for her own desperate sorrow.

Guilt lay heavily on Laine's chest, and she wished she could erase the terrible feelings of anger and envy she'd felt too often in years past. Her bitter, jealous words aimed at her younger sister weighed on her shoulders like a hulking beast.

Pushing the memories aside, Laine rose from the chair and drained the last swallow of her cold coffee. After setting the cup in the sink, she turned, braced her back against the kitchen counter, and again regarded the golden flecks of sunlight blinking on the lake. Air is what she needed. Fresh air and a few moments to calm her pulsing heart.

A rowboat tied to the small wooden dock bobbed in the morning sunlight. Why not? Since she'd moved back to Michigan and into the condominium a week earlier, she hadn't gone near the water except for the day she was guided through the rental by the agent. Adjusting to her new position at Artistic Interiors and organizing her belongings had taken all her time. On her first free Sunday morning, she could use a distraction, something pleasant like a few relaxing moments on the lake.

Pulling her makeup bag from her purse, she glimpsed in the hall mirror and dashed frosty orange lipstick along the bow of her lips. Scrutinizing her appearance, she decided she'd do. Who would she impress this early in the morning anyway? People with any sense at all were still dawdling on the edge of sleep.

Stepping onto her screened porch, she locked the condo door and dropped the key into the pocket of her walking shorts. The oars lay along the porch wall, and she grabbed them and maneuvered the pair through the doorway and down the two steps to the outside. As she marched toward the path leading to the dock, she heard the screen door swish closed behind her.

When Laine reached the water, a warm June breeze curled along her bare skin, and her sneakers gripped the rough dock boards with a punctuating thud. The small rowboat appeared safe enough, so she slid the paddles into the oarlocks. Grabbing the side of the boat, Laine slipped off the rope tethering the stern, then holding the boat fast, she inched her way forward toward the front mooring.

As she clutched the dock pole, she edged one foot into the dinghy, but the momentum shifted the rowboat from the pier. With a gasp, she clutched the mooring to no avail. The dinghy continued its journey while her yell echoed across the quiet water and she clung to the piling with her left foot on the dock and her right foot in the drifting boat.

As the inevitable rose to meet her, a strong masculine voice struck her ear. "Hang on."

But his encouragement came too late, and she belly-flopped into the cold, sea-weedy water. As she bobbed to the surface, smiling hazel eyes greeted her, and she heard the same full-throated voice. "Good morning. Decided to take an early dip, I see."

"Decided isn't quite the word," Laine muttered as he reached out to her. She grasped his hand, and with one heave, he lifted her, dripping with water and greenish-brown seaweed, to the dock.

When she had the courage to look at him, his amusement sent her mortification packing. She laughed at herself and her wasted effort, recalling the feeble swipe of lipstick moments earlier.

"Nice to see you have a sense of humor," he said. But his expression became serious as he eyed her from head to toe. "Anything hurt?"

"Only my pride." Laine extended her brackish hand. "Thanks for the save. I'm Laine Sibley."

"Laine. Nice name." His lightly stubbled square jaw returned to its friendly smile. "I'm Jeff. Jeff Rice, your neighbor."

With her humiliation in check, Laine focused on the good-looking man standing beside her. A rust-colored knit shirt stretched across his broad chest and hung partway down his beige-colored swim trunks. A full head of tawny hair lay in casual waves that framed his square face. Raising her eyes to his, she caught a flash of curiosity.

"Well, that's it for a relaxing drift on the lake," she said. "The algae and I should go rinse off."

He caught his belt loop with his thumb and glanced across the once-again undisturbed lake. "Why miss the boat ride? I'll wait while you clean up and keep you company. . .unless you'd rather go out alone." He paused.

Laine took a faltering step backward. "No, I'll—" She glanced toward the condo. "I'll be only a couple of minutes." She swung around and dashed up the walk.

Jeff grinned as the attractive blond trotted up the walk, leaving a wet trail behind her. Despite the mermaid disguise, her beauty was evident. When he'd come to her rescue, her peacock blue eyes caught him off guard. When she bobbed to the surface, his heart skipped a beat. Add to those eyes her smooth creamy skin and bowed lips, and her face resembled the antique China doll he'd found in his mother's attic after she'd died.

The memory tightened his belly, and he pushed the thought aside and refocused on the woman he'd just met. Delicate featured, yes, but he sensed she was no fragile toy. Her broad shoulders tapering to strong legs disclosed the body of a capable athlete. Swimmer, he guessed.

Admiring her, he jolted when she turned around and darted back down the path.

"My key," she called, pointing to the lake.

A moment passed before he understood. When her foot sounded on the wooden boards, he was already peering into the dark water, hoping to catch the glint of her key in the shadows.

"How stupid." She knelt beside him, squinting into the water. "See anything? I had it in my pocket."

His vision sought the murky lake bottom. "Only a key?"

"On a chain," she answered.

Something pale glinted beneath the surface. "Is there white on the chain?"

"Uh-huh. Do you see it?"

"I think so." He hadn't anticipated jumping into the shore water, preferring the clearer water by the raft, but how could he ignore a woman in distress? He rose and tugged the knit shirt over his head.

As if understanding his action, she bolted up. "No, I'm already wet and dirty. Show me where, and I'll get it."

He ignored her plea, but before he could stop her, she leaped into the murky water with him. Grabbing the key chain from the sludgy bottom, he rose to the surface. Below in the water, her honey-colored hair splayed about her like silken threads.

When she bounced upward, she peered at him, then at the chain dangling from his fingers. "Why did you do that? I didn't want you to get wet."

"No problem." He forced a gallant pose. "I'd planned to swim anyway, but from the raft." He stared off at the sparkling water further out in the lake, then handed her the key with a chuckle. "Now, if you'd still like to go for that boat ride, I'll meet you back here in a couple of minutes."

❧

The dip of the oars rippled the deep green water and broke the silence. Laine studied Jeff's iron-clad midriff as it tensed and relaxed with the pull of the oars. He wasn't a tall man, under six feet she guessed, but he was strong and solid. Yet his kindness—more like chivalry—was what she found most appealing. Gentle control. His bronzed body flexed, and her curiosity won the battle. "Do you work out?"

He squinted toward her into the sunlight. "Not much. You?"

"Me?" She chuckled. "Not really. I jog and swim, but that's about it. My stationary bike makes a great clothes valet."

"You too?"

"So then, what do you do to keep yourself in shape?"

His face flashed surprise but in a heartbeat shifted to a grin. "My job, I suppose."

Wondering what made him flinch, she asked, "What do you do for a living?"

"Troubleshooter," he said, staring off in the distance. "Computers."

"Troubleshooter, huh? I'd guess something more exciting and dangerous."

Jerking his head back toward her, he grinned. "Like alligator wrestling?"

"No." Laine laughed, but she had to admit to herself that wrestling seemed more like it. Computers didn't fit. "More like, Superman."

Jeff shook his head. "Nope. I'm much more boring than Clark Kent. So how about you?"

"Commercial interior design. I moved here from Chicago last week to work with a Bloomfield Hills company. We design decor for businesses, restaurants, hotels, corporate offices."

"You're from Chicago, then?"

"Not really. Michigan's my home."

"Come clean. You were homesick. Am I right?"

His comments dragged her stifled feelings to the surface. "My younger sister's ill, and. . .I thought I should be nearby."

Shifting with discomfort, Jeff let the oars drag in the water. "I'm sorry. It's serious?"

"Cancer." The word knotted in her throat. "Both our parents died from the same."

Silence hung on the warm breeze. A dog's bark echoed across the water, and in the distance, the rumble of a motor swept in, then drifted off on the air.

He averted his eyes, gazing somewhere beyond her. "Mine are both dead too. I'm it." He shrugged and gave the oars a hefty pull. "What you see is what you get."

His words rattled in her thoughts, and she glanced at her wristwatch. "I'd better get back. I promised Kathleen I'd stop by, and she's probably looking for me—not to mention her daughter, Becca. She's my cutie of a niece."

"How old is she? Your niece, I mean." Without question, Jeff pivoted the rowboat back toward shore.

"Just turned five. My heart breaks thinking about what she'll face if something happens to my sister." When something happens. Laine swallowed back the thought and focused on the shoreline closing in on them. "I'm sorry I got morbid. I've had all this pressing on my mind."

"No problem. That's what ears are for—to listen. Once in awhile I've wished someone had listened to me."

His mouth closed, and she didn't have the nerve to ask what he meant. When the boat thudded against the dock, they climbed out and tied it to the pilings, then parted, each going in their own direction. But as Laine dressed to visit her sister, Jeff's image remained in her thoughts.

❧

Laine heard Becca's eager squeal before she saw her.

"Auntie Laine." The petite, fair-skinned, dark-haired child darted through the doorway. The bang of the screen door echoed as Becca bounded into Laine's opened arms.

"Hi, Sweetie." Laine nuzzled her face in the child's silky cheek. "I've missed you."

"Me too. Mama's waiting for you."

"I know."

Becca snuggled a battered rag doll against her chest, but she grabbed Laine's hand and led her into the pleasant Cape Cod, its white siding trimmed with dark gray shutters.

Inside, Kathleen lay propped against a pile of colorful pillows on the living-room sofa. Her gaunt skin looked the color of bleached ash, a sad contrast to her bright surroundings. Her attempt at a smile broke Laine's heart.

"How you doing, Sis?" Laine asked, leaning over to kiss her sister's cheek. "I see Mrs. Dexter got you all gussied up." Laine crossed the beige carpet and plopped into a nearby chair.

Kathleen shifted her gaze toward Laine. "I don't think 'gussied' is the word, but she tried." A meager chuckle followed her words.

Laine struggled to keep her voice steady as she noticed her sister's glazed eyes. "It's good to see you dressed and out of bed. Did you have lunch?"

Kathleen nodded. "Mavis fixed some soup, but Becca wouldn't eat. She said you'd take her for fast food." The last words faded like the end of an echo.

Laine forced a cheery laugh, but inside her heart cried. Her sister couldn't last much longer. The look seemed too familiar. Her memory took her back to her parents' deaths—each different, yet each the same.

"I'll take Becca to lunch in a little bit. I thought I'd spend a few minutes with you for a change." A few minutes. How could she cover so many years in minutes? Thinking back, so much had happened. And so much more would happen now—with the horrible illness pulling Kathleen's world apart. They had so much to talk about, but for Laine, facing it gave the future too much unwanted reality.

Every time they were together, Laine hoped she could ask the right questions and get the needed answers. Her first concern was Becca. What did Kathleen have planned for the child's care? What about Becca's paternal grandmother, Glynnis Keary? Had Kathleen contacted her? And finally, how much money had Kathleen been able to rescue from the man who'd walked into her life after Alex's tragic death? The queries tore through Laine, striking the brick wall of her cowardice. And worse, she faced her own need to ask Kathleen's forgiveness.

"I'm so glad you have Mrs. Dexter, Kath," Laine said.

"She's a real godsend."

"Like a mother." Her words faded.

Laine studied her face, seeing the evidence of pain pulling at every muscle. "Is it time for your medication? Where is it?"

Kathleen tilted her head toward the table, and Laine grabbed the pills and poured water into a glass from the pitcher. She rested her sister's head in her arm and eased the water between her dried lips until Kathleen swallowed the pill.

Desperation washed over Laine. The time had come. Now or never. She saw it in every detail of her sister's appearance. But how to begin.

"Remember when we were kids?" Laine said, delving into her memories. "We had some good times. I often think of the vacations we had. I always smile when I think of the cottage Dad rented. I suppose that's why I moved into a condo on the lake. Such great memories." For a moment, her grief dissipated as nostalgia bathed her in warm thoughts. "Remember fishing, Sis? Dad would take us out in the boat. . .and before your worm hit the water, you were asking if you'd caught a fish." Laine grinned with the reminiscence. "Then when you finally caught a bluegill, you were so excited. We'd have thought you'd caught a whale."

A faint grin stirred Kathleen's mouth. "A—And your first . . .date, remem. . ."

Laine sank with the ache that lodged in her heart. "How could I forget? You pouted because you had to stay home." The scene rolled in as tears rimmed Laine's lashes. "My date. . . What was his name? Mike Bennett, I think. Anyway, he thought you were so cute." She touched Kathleen's arm. "I never told you, but he said you could come along with us." The confession triggered her shame. Everyone thought Kathleen was cute—beautiful when she matured. And Laine had been envious. Always.

"C—Christmases," Kathleen whispered. "R—remember. . .

my doll?" She struggled to speak while anguish rifled across her face.

Covering her despair, Laine pushed a chuckle from her chest. "I do. I told Mom and Dad I was too grown-up for a doll, but when Christmas arrived. . .I wanted a doll just like the one they'd given you."

Kathleen nodded. A tear dripped from her lashes and rolled down her cheek. "Good times, Laine."

Laine studied her sister's face. Tell her. Tell her before it's too late. She closed her eyes, begging for a way to empty her mind of guilt and sorrow. But who was she begging? God? God had faded from her life so long ago. A ragged breath escaped her lips. "Kathleen, can you hear me?"

Her sister's eyes opened and closed. A faint nod answered her question.

"I need to talk with you before. . ." Laine paused and tried again. "For so many years I've been weighted with guilt, I don't even know where to begin."

Kathleen shifted her hand toward Laine's, her mouth opening and closing in silence.

Laine covered her sister's icy hand. "Don't try to talk, Sis. Just listen." Once more, Laine dragged strength from somewhere inside. "I've spent my life envying you. You were more beautiful, more talented, and worst of all, more lucky. Blessed, Mom and Dad called it."

Kathleen's eyes fluttered, focusing for a heartbeat before they closed.

"I seemed to struggle for everything, while you. . .seemed to be covered in good fortune. . .and I prayed, Kathleen, that you'd learn a little about suffering."

Laine's voice broke, and tears spilled from her eyes like the shame that overflowed her heart. Without stopping, she whispered the story of her jealousy, the prayers for retribution, the guilt when Kathleen's husband died as if a vengeful God had answered her prayers. She'd even begrudged Kathleen her baby daughter. "I can't ask for your forgiveness. What I felt all those years is unforgivable, but if I could go back and erase the past, I would. I've missed you so much, but my bitterness and envy. . .and then my shame kept me away."

Kathleen's eyes opened. Mingled in the pain, compassion shone through. "N–No need to for–give. I've al–ways loved—you."

Despair knotted Laine's chest and weighed against her stomach. Grief rose in her throat like bile. She longed to embrace her sister, to hold her against her chest, to crush away the pain Kathleen had lived with for years. Pain? Laine didn't know pain. Today she saw it—the agony of death—in Kathleen's face. "I love you, Sis."

They sat silently for a moment until Kathleen struggled to open her eyes briefly as she whispered words Laine didn't want to hear. "It's time for hospice, Laine. They'll help all of us." Her eyes drifted closed again, and Laine stood above her, watching her even, shallow breathing.

With Kathleen resting, Laine wiped the tears clinging to her lashes, then peeked into the kitchen where Mavis Dexter entertained Becca. "I gave Kathleen her pain medication, and she's sleeping. I think Becca and I'll go have some lunch." She sent a tired grin to the elderly woman who was sipping from a cup clutched in her gnarled hands.

"Good. The child's been waiting for you all day." Mavis's pale blue eyes looked as weary and spent as Laine's tethered emotions made her feel.

Becca jumped from the chair and wrapped her dainty fingers around Laine's. "Burger Barn, okay? And I'll bring Penny, too."

"Burger Barn it is, Becca. And you know your dolly's invited."

Becca tucked her rag doll under her arm, and they tiptoed

past Kathleen and headed out the front door. Laine glanced one last time over her shoulder at her sleeping sister, wishing she'd had the courage to talk long ago. Now they would have to fit a lifetime of communication into a few final hours.

two

Sitting across from Becca at Burger Barn, Laine studied her niece's deep blue eyes, pale with sadness. Though the child bubbled with talk about the toy she'd found in the fast food's special Kiddie's Lunch Bag, Laine recognized an underlining fear that found its way into the child's face.

Love filled Laine's heart as she regarded the lovely child. Her dark curls haloed her fair face, and Mavis had dressed her in a yellow-and-blue-striped top that gave her a cheery look, belying the trying times she faced.

What could she do for this little girl? She'd asked herself the question too many times since she'd left Kathleen's side. Becca would soon need someone to offer her love, support, and understanding when her mother was gone. Worry and sadness pushed behind Laine's eyes, and despite her attempts to control them, tears clung to her lashes.

"Did you get something in your eye, Auntie?" Becca asked, studying her face with a child's curiosity.

Laine brushed away the moisture with her fingers. "I think I did, Sweetie." She and Becca needed to talk. Though only five, the child would soon face adult decisions—changes in her life no little girl should have to deal with.

In the silent lull, Becca's expression shifted to sadness. She tilted her head up, looking into Laine's eyes again. . .for tears perhaps. Studying the child, Laine wondered if Becca wanted permission to shed her own tears.

"Are you worried about your mom?" Laine asked, reaching across the table to hold the child's hand.

Becca nodded. "Mommy tells me not to worry. She says

Jesus is always by my side to help me."

The child's words rolled through Laine's thoughts. "Then you should listen to your mom, Becca."

"Jesus is by your side too, Auntie. Mom said He's like our shadow. Wherever we go, we have a friend who goes with us."

A shadow. God had been a shadow to Laine for many years. Not Becca's kind of shadow, but a dark, undefined shape that she could never touch. "That's a nice thought," she said, wishing the shadow offered her the same comfort it seemed to give Becca.

"I have a picture book with Jesus holding open His arms to all the children. Know what He says?" Her face brightened.

Laine remembered the story from her own childhood. " 'Suffer the little children to come unto me, and forbid them not.' Is that right?"

Becca smiled and nodded, but Laine's thoughts settled on the word "suffer." She had suffered for years, and now Becca would suffer. What kind of God causes little children to suffer? As the question rose in her mind, her thoughts flew to the end of the verse: *Whosoever shall not receive the kingdom of God as a little child, shall in no wise enter therein.* Becca accepted God's Word just as Laine had done as a child. Had that been her flaw these past years? Had she been seeking explanations and answers that a finite mind couldn't understand? Had her heart closed to accepting God without question. Sadly, she knew the answer.

She harnessed the pressing questions and drew her attention back to Becca. "I'm glad you can turn to Jesus, Becca. We all need someone to turn to when we're confused or—"

"I don't want Mommy to be sick."

Her statement jolted Laine's emotions. "I don't either, Sweetheart. I'd give so much if your mom was well."

"Auntie," Becca said, looking like a child who'd been caught doing mischief. "Even though Jesus is my friend, I want my mommy to be with me too." Her voice caught in her throat. "Sometimes, I'm afraid."

Laine squeezed her hand, wondering if she should tell the little girl her own feelings. "I know, Becca. I wish I could tell you things will be all right, but—"

"Is Mommy going to die?" Fear filled the child's eyes.

Laine's heart sank. She couldn't lie. . .yet she didn't want to frighten her niece any more than she was already. "Only God can answer that," she said, surprising herself by alluding to the Lord.

"I asked God to take care of her," Becca said. Her face twisted with a new thought. "God takes care of my daddy in heaven. That's what Mommy says."

"God's children live with Him on earth and in heaven, Becca, so you can be sure that He'll take care of your mom." *God's children?* Laine heard the words and wished she felt like one of God's children instead of like an unforgivable sinner.

Pulling her thoughts away from her selfish concerns, Laine focused on Becca. How could she help the child through the grief she would soon face when her own sorrow covered her mind like a shroud? "No matter what happens, your mom will be with Jesus. . .and no matter what happens, you have people who love you."

Becca studied the trinket from her lunch bag, then lifted her head. "You love me, and Mavis does too."

Her heart in her throat, Laine moved around the table to be closer to the child and wrapped her arms around her thin shoulders. "Everyone who knows you loves you, Sweetie. Mavis loves you. . .and I love you more than words can say." She rested her head on Becca's soft, dark curls, commanding her tears to stay behind her eyes.

Today she could not worry about her own sins or faults. Today her concern was for the child. A child who had more confidence in and understanding of God than Laine had gained in a lifetime.

❧

The visit with Kathleen and Becca had drained Laine. Emotionally overwrought, she sat staring across the tranquil lake. Not one wave ruffled the water, and the still water washed her in a gentle calm.

Bitterness that lay bound in Laine's heart for years had tied her spirit in knots, causing her to question so many things about herself and her worth. Since appearing back in Kathleen's life, Laine had let the bitterness seep away, and today her confession had loosened her guilt—not released it totally so it could drift away but eased it so that only slender threads linked it to her soul.

She'd longed for forgiveness. But today, a new reality overwhelmed her. Though Kathleen had whispered her forgiveness, Laine could not accept the gift and forgive herself. She prayed in time she would, but the longing seemed like a vague dream.

The peacefulness of the lake washed over her thoughts, calming her in its silver stillness. The outdoors beckoned, and remembering her earlier dunking, Laine headed for the bedroom to change. A real swim might relax her.

After slipping into her apple green swimsuit, she grabbed a towel and headed outdoors. She studied the rowboat, wondering if she could maneuver it this time without another catastrophe. With greater care, she successfully climbed in and rowed to the wooden raft resting on four large empty oil drums a hundred yards from shore.

She tethered the boat and climbed onto the raft. Tossing her towel on the wooden planks, Laine dove into the deep green water. For a moment, a chill ran through her, but by the time she surfaced, the water felt pleasant and refreshing in the late afternoon sun.

Like a fish, she glided along in the water, her arms cutting through the quiet bracing ripples. When she slowed and sighted the raft two hundred yards behind her, she jack-knifed her legs and headed back. After she lifted herself up the two wooden steps, she dabbed the towel on her damp skin, then spread the terry cloth out like a blanket. Stretched out on her belly, she rested her head, using her hands for a pillow, and breathed deeply, sensing the water's calming effect.

The raft gave a sudden dip and bob. Laine opened her eyes, startled by the movement. A shadow fell across the wooden planks, and she lifted her head to see a pair of powerful arms gripping the ladder top. In one smooth motion, they pulled a solid torso of bronzed muscle to the wooden deck. Jeff stood above her, his hazel eyes reflecting the green of the water. "You're doing it right this time, huh?"

She raised herself on her elbows. "Right?"

"Bathing suit, towel, the works."

Laine grinned and rolled on her side, pulling her legs around to a seated position. "This is a comparison test. I want to see which method is best."

"And?"

The sun glinted over his shoulder, and she squinted up at him. "I haven't quite made up my mind. But I'm leaning toward a planned dip."

"Good thinking. Mind if I join you?"

His grin ruffled her pulse, and if she were candid, she'd tell him he was the best thing that had happened to her that day. "Raft belongs to everyone. But I'd enjoy the company."

He lowered himself beside her on the bare wood and ran his fingers over his stubbled chin. "Bad day with your sister?"

Laine nodded. "It's heavy stuff. Weighs on the heart, you know, watching her suffer and seeing Becca's fear. And I'm such a coward."

"Coward?" His smooth forehead wrinkled with question. "Why?"

"Because we need to talk. So many things to discuss and so much I'd like to say, but I just can't bring myself to do it."

He stared at his feet. "I don't think you're a coward." He lifted his gaze to hers. "You're human. I'd feel the same way."

Something about his manner calmed Laine, an understanding or compassion she didn't see often in others, especially a near stranger. But his manner soothed her, drew her out, and she fought to keep her emotions in check. She felt a strong desire to pour her burdens out to him like a patient would to her doctor.

She studied his interesting face, noting the facial hair that had caught her attention earlier. "Is that beard coming or ready to take a hike?"

He chuckled good-naturedly. "Coming, but I'm thinking of ditching it. Thought I'd give it a try, but maybe summer isn't the best time."

"I suppose." She studied his jaw, envisioning him smooth shaven. "In case I don't recognize you if you decide to shave, yell out your name, okay?"

"I'll do that." A grin played on his lips.

"The swim felt good," Laine said after a lengthy silence. "Relaxing."

He didn't respond; instead he studied her face. "You look more relaxed than earlier today."

She sensed he wanted to say something further, but he remained silent, and she struggled to think of something to talk about. Silence wasn't golden to her. But before she'd come up with a new topic, he spoke.

"Swimming always feels good. But you know what else would feel even better?"

Laine's head jerked up, and she stared at him. Her stomach knotted in disappointment. A come-on. It hadn't entered her mind. "No, what?" She heard the tension in her voice.

A smile curled his lips as if he read her mind. "A nice steak dinner. I just happen to have a couple of thick, juicy T-bones waiting for two hungry swimmers."

She felt a heated flush rise up her neck to her cheeks, and watching his expression, he hadn't missed its journey. "Two steaks?" She shook her head. "Sorry. My thoughts were way off base."

"I noticed." His chuckle was hearty. "I'm not your local masher. Really. I'm a pretty nice guy when you get to know me."

"I'm surprised you'd want to know me after detecting my evil thoughts."

"Hey, a girl has to protect herself. A steak is what I had in mind. Grilled any way you like it."

"How about medium rare, sort of the shade of pink my face was a few minutes ago?"

His laughter drifted to her ears like music.

❧

Jeff closed up the grill and carried the last of the dishes into the kitchen. He'd filled Laine's glass with iced tea, and she sat on a canvas chair on the front lawn, facing the vanishing sun. Grabbing a drink for himself, he joined her, and they sat silently focused on the golden ball as it dropped behind the trees, leaving purple and orange tails tangled in the distant foliage like the remnants of a kite.

A soft sigh touched his ear, and he turned with interest to the gentle sound. "Now did I keep my word?"

"Better than your word. Great steak and friendly conversation. Couldn't ask for more."

"That's the way it should be."

She shifted in her chair and turned toward him, wrapping her fingers around the honey-colored tresses that curled to her shoulders. With a gentle motion, she flicked the hair behind her and tilted her head. "So you've heard pieces of my sad story. Tell me about you."

"You'd be bored out of your mind."

"That's what I need. Maybe I'd have a good night's sleep, reminiscing about our conversation."

Her teasing smile tickled him, and for once, he wished he could be honest and tell her about his life. But that wasn't possible.

He pushed the real Jeff back and instead told her a mixture of truth and fiction. "Oh, after some college and. . .special training, I started work, but a desk job didn't interest me. I needed something more lively. So when the troubleshooting opportunity came along, I took it. I guess that's it." He paused, though her face disclosed she wanted more.

"Marriage? Children?" she asked.

"Neither fit into my plans really well." He looked away, uncomfortable, but she'd asked, and he felt compelled to answer. "I was engaged for awhile to a nice Christian woman, but her needs and mine sort of hit a fork in the road. It seemed for the best."

Her face brightened with his words. "You're a Christian?"

Squirming at her question, he shrugged. "I believe in God. I know Jesus died for my sins, but I guess it bogs down there. Too many things in my life that I question. Not who God is, but why God lets things happen. Haven't quite resolved it all yet." He looked into her eyes. "Does that disappoint you?"

She gazed across the water in silence. When she finally answered, her tone said more than her words—telling and sad. "Not disappointment. You've echoed my own feelings. I believe, but I've drifted too. I grew up going to church and Sunday school. I know Jesus came to earth to save sinners and offer forgiveness. But somehow I feel. . .I need to forgive myself first." Her gaze drifted to his. "Remember the Lord's Prayer? How can I ask to be forgiven if I haven't done the same?" Her lovely blue eyes were heavy with questions.

He considered her words. What did she mean, "forgive myself first?" For what? He wanted to make some kind of statement, but the words tangled in his mind.

"Don't try to answer. I have to do that for myself."

He closed his mouth. She'd guessed right. Words from years back jumped to his tongue ready to exit, but he tucked them inside. The Bible said to repent and be saved. As far as he was concerned, if anyone were repentant, she surely was.

"Enough about me," she said. "Back to you. What happened to your parents?"

Her question bunched inside his head like knotted threads, and he pulled strands of memories apart to find an answer. "My father died ten years ago when I was twenty-four. Heart attack. My mom. . ." His throat constricted, and he swallowed. "My mom died suddenly four years later." His thoughts lifted heavenward like a prayer. *No details, please.*

"That was pretty close together. My dad lived about ten years after my mom," Laine said. "He was twelve years older. She was only thirty-nine when she died."

Slowly, she sipped her tea, then staring at the glass in her hand, she circled its rim with her index finger. "There must be something more pleasant we can talk about." She glanced at her wristwatch and rose. "But. . .I'd really better get going." She set the glass on a small wooden folding table. "Tomorrow's a workday, and I don't know about you, but I'm under the gun learning the quirks of a new company." She grinned. "They call it protocol."

Jeff controlled a nervous chuckle. She'd struck closer to home than she knew. "I've been under the gun myself a few times."

She turned to him with her hand extended. "Thanks for the great dinner, Jeff, and the company. I needed a lift today."

As he grasped her hand, she sputtered a laugh. "Especially this morning. Thanks for giving me a lift twice."

His thoughts sailed back to the morning when he'd first glimpsed her peacock blue eyes set in a very surprised and wet face. "Anytime," he said, fighting the desire to touch her soft cheek in the dusky light.

෪

Becca hung onto Laine's porch door, her nose pressed against the screen. "When can we go swimming? You promised. Remember?"

Laine's spirit lifted, seeing her niece focused on play. "Where's your patience?"

"What?" Becca asked, releasing the door and turning to face Laine.

"Patience," she repeated. "Your. . ." She grasped for a simple definition and found none. "Your ability to wait a few minutes." Looking at the child more closely, Laine chuckled and walked across the room to brush the mesh-shaped patch of dust from the end of Becca's nose. "And with a smile."

Becca ran the back of her hand over the same spot, then sent her a silly grin. "I can smile."

"But can you smile and wait?"

Giggles burst from Becca's throat.

"Remember? We just had lunch." She gave Becca a hug and patted her belly. "Didn't your mom tell you to wait an hour before going in the water?" As soon as the question left her, Laine wished she'd not mentioned Kathleen.

Becca shook her head. "We don't have water at our house."

Relieved the girl hadn't been troubled by the reference to her mother, Laine ran her hand along the length of Becca's curls. "How about this? You can get on your bathing suit and play outside."

"Yippee!" she squealed.

Laine tilted Becca's chin and aimed her eyes at hers. "But on the hill, not by the water."

"I promise," Becca said, skipping toward the guest room,

where she had dumped her sack of toys and a clean change of clothes.

Laine returned to her job in the kitchen, and when Becca passed on her way outside, she reminded her to stay on the hill. When she'd loaded the dishwasher and wiped the countertop, Laine grabbed a soda and headed for the porch to check up on her charge.

Having a child around the house seemed strange. But a good kind of strange. Becca's chatter and inquisitive nature kept Laine on her toes, always trying to stay one step ahead of the child's imagination.

In the living room, Laine heard Becca's voice through the open door. Talking to the rag doll, Laine thought, recalling that the worn-out toy always seemed anchored to Becca's side. Where she went, Penny followed.

When Laine reached the porch, Jeff's voice rose from beneath the screen windows.

Pressing her nose against the screen, Laine peeked below the sill. Jeff sat cross-legged on the grass, deep in conversation with Becca.

"I wondered who she was talking with," Laine said.

Jeff tilted back his head and grinned. "We're discussing important things. Care to join us?"

Laine pushed open the screen door and stepped outside. "Becca, this is my neighbor, J—"

"Jeff," Becca said, in a tone that told Laine she considered herself in control of the situation. "We introduced ourselves."

"Ah, you introduced yourselves. That's good manners." Controlling a grin, Laine folded her arms and gave Becca a wink. "Becca's spending the day with me."

Jeff rose and brushed the grass from his beige shorts. "You're a lucky woman. I can tell already that Becca's a special young lady."

A grin spread across his face as he lifted his finger and

brushed a smudge of window-screen dust from the end of Laine's nose.

"Dirt?" she asked.

He nodded.

"You'd think I'd have learned."

His puzzled expression caused her to explain.

"Becca tells me you're going for a swim," Jeff said, giving Laine a stealthy wink. "Good fun. . .and a healthy distraction."

Laine nodded, knowing he remembered Becca's predicament.

"What's a distraction?" Becca asked.

"You are, my pretty," Jeff said, clasping her under the arms and swinging her in the air.

"Me?" she giggled.

When he lowered her to the ground, she gazed at him with admiration. "Can you swim with us too?"

"If your aunt invites me."

"Auntie?" she pleaded, her eyes widening.

"Why not?" She gave Jeff a poke. "Keeping my eye on two kids shouldn't be any harder than one."

The joke flew far above Becca's head while Jeff gave Laine's arm a playful squeeze.

"I'll run back and put on my trunks." Facing forward, he moved away from them in a backward trot. "And maybe we could take out that old rowboat. I bet Becca would like to give it a spin."

The child's head bounced like a buckboard on a corduroy road.

With a contented sigh, Laine stepped back into the house, more than grateful for Jeff's kindness. With his tender disposition, Jeff seemed like a man who should have kids of his own. He'd be a great father.

❧

The thick carpet hushed Laine's footsteps as she entered her office the next morning. She yawned, standing beside her desk. During the night, sleep had evaded her. When her mind hadn't been weaving through questions about Becca's future, it had been riveted to thoughts of her neighbor's warm, friendly eyes.

Noticing the time, Laine gathered her folders and headed for the conference room. Since starting this new job, she'd learned she could count on the company's traditional Monday morning strategy meeting.

When she slipped into the room, she greeted her new acquaintances and slid into the same chair she'd used the first Monday she'd been with the company.

Hanging on the periphery of casual conversation, Laine doodled on her legal pad before the meeting began, but the random scrawls transformed into a list of the questions and concerns that had lingered in her thoughts during her sleepless night. Though she'd confessed her past issues with Kathleen, she vowed today they must deal with other pressing concerns. Especially her worry about Becca's future.

The meeting began, and Laine struggled to keep her mind alert to the various topics as the discussion bounced around the room. As the meeting drew to a close, the door inched open, and a secretary tiptoed into the room and slipped a telephone memo in front of Laine. The word "emergency" leaped from the pink paper, and without a word of explanation, she gathered her folders and left the room, her heart pounding in her ears.

At the first available telephone, Laine listened to Mrs. Dexter's narrative of Kathleen's condition. Within minutes, Laine had left the building and headed for St. John's emergency room. Her fingers gripped the steering wheel, and tears blurred the traffic lights as she maneuvered her way through the late-morning traffic.

Arriving in ER, Laine followed a nurse's directions to Kathleen's bedside. She stood above her sister, who had been wired and tubed to flashing machinery and dripping bags, and chastised herself for waiting too long.

When Kathleen's groggy eyes drifted open, her whisper rose to Laine's waiting ears. "I'm not going anywhere, Laine, until we talk."

Unable to speak, Laine could only squeeze her hand.

"Don't say. . .a word. Just listen," Kathleen murmured. Drifting in and out of sleep, she dragged sentence fragments from between her lips. "I've put your name on my bank account. . .and as beneficiary to. . .everything." She dragged in a breath, her face twisting in agony. "What's important. . .what I must know is. . .if you'll take care of Becca." For a heartbeat her clouded eyes cleared, their look piercing Laine's.

Laine swallowed the emotion that rose to her throat. Becca? She loved the child, but how could she care for her? Her work often meant late hours. Yet the look on her sister's pain-wracked face knifed through her, and she nodded.

"Say it, Laine. Promise me."

Laine couldn't remember the last time she'd prayed, but her heart lifted in prayer, begging God for wisdom. "I promise, Kath. I love Becca with all my heart."

Kathleen's rigid shoulders sank into the pillows, and her face filled with peace. "Thank you."

Laine backed into a lone chair next to the bed and collapsed, her knees shaking from the weight of her promise. If God could work a miracle, she'd give anything to have Kathleen rouse and heal. But reality smacked her between the eyes.

Gazing at her sister's tired, illness-strained face, Laine's thoughts drifted back to when Kathleen's rosy cheeks and sky blue eyes captured the hearts of every man she met. While Laine was plowing through her senior year of college, Kathleen had hired in as a secretary at Keary Investments, and within a year, she'd swept the young heir apparent off his feet.

Despite the Keary family's disapproval, Kathleen had eloped with Alexander Keary, only their witnesses in attendance at the wedding service. They'd shocked not only Laine and her father, but they'd also destroyed the dreams of the Keary family. They'd expected their son to marry someone with their social prominence, not a naive teenager who'd graduated only from high school.

Laine had struggled with her envy for years. Though she had been born with some of the family's good looks, her sister seemed to float above the world on ethereal loveliness and good luck. Without struggling through college, Kathleen had gained a rich and handsome husband, a beautiful home, and then a beautiful baby daughter.

About the time Laine had graduated from college, her father died, leaving a few bills and no inheritance that mattered. Laine lived in her cramped apartment, working her way up through the ranks of commercial designers, fighting her way through the backbiting world of work, wishing her sister knew a little pain.

Laine's wish rose like a dragon when Alex was killed in a small plane crash on the way home from a business trip. Kathleen was left with a young child and a large inheritance. Yet Laine had envied her the child and the money. And then the dragon's hot breath had seared Kathleen's life again in the form of Scott Derian. Scott had charmed his way into Kathleen's life, swindling her out of much of her fortune. As mysteriously as he'd sailed in, he'd sailed out again, leaving her with little, from what Laine could calculate. Kathleen was reluctant to admit much of anything in the aftermath of that relationship.

And now, once again, Laine looked into Kathleen's face and wished with all her heart that she hadn't allowed bitterness and envy to keep them apart.

"Laine."

Laine pulled herself from her thoughts. Had Kathleen spoken or had it been a dream? "Kathleen?"

Her sister's eyes fluttered. "I must tell you. . ." Her voice faded, drifting back into a drugged sleep.

Laine focused on the lights flashing around her sister's bedside and listened to the steady pump and hiss of the machinery. The bedsheet rose and fell in imperceptible, uneven flutters. Laine slid her hand to Kathleen's cold, still fingers, covering them with her own and closing her eyes.

What must Kathleen tell her? She watched her sister through a blur of tears, wondering what she could do for Becca. The child needed time and attention, and all she had to give her was love. Her mind flew to Glynnis Keary, Alex's mother. She should be told about Kathleen's illness. She would want to give Becca the best. This subject was the final thing Laine needed to discuss with Kathleen.

"Kathleen," Laine whispered. Her sister didn't stir, looking at rest. More peaceful than Laine had seen her in days. Then Laine's focus flew to the straight line on the monitor and the still, unmoving white shroud that covered her sister's withered frame.

Behind Laine's eyes the torrent gathered, pressing into the corners and along the rim of her lashes, then dripping to her hands. Laine lifted her blurred vision to Kathleen's peaceful face. Her heart stood still for one breathless moment as reality knotted within her.

Becca.

three

Heavyhearted, Laine slid another carton onto the stack and wandered through the empty house. Even with the furniture removed—sold to a used furniture store—the house still radiated Kathleen's personality. Laine scanned the rooms, admiring the flowered borders rimming the ceilings and lending a hue to the painted walls. Color and cheer. She envisioned the joy that had once been Kathleen's before Alex died.

Painfully, she'd boxed Kathleen's clothing. Mavis's church sent a van to pick up the donation for their distribution center. Laine had only kept trinkets, jewelry boxes, and other personal items that she thought Becca might be pleased to have when she grew older.

Laine had wept as she and Jeff had dismantled Becca's bedroom and loaded it into a rental truck to move to her condo. What would Laine do now? Could she handle the needs of a five-year-old girl when she barely had a grip on her own emotional demands?

Again Mavis had been a blessing. She'd taken Becca into her home for two days while the contents of the house had been packed and dispersed. Though she was grateful to Mavis, Laine worried that Becca would again feel abandoned since she wasn't there for the child. But the work had to be done, and allowing Becca to watch the dismantling of her home seemed even worse to Laine.

Though Kathleen's death had been horrible for Becca, her mother's funeral had added to the toll. The utter finality of the service left the child despondent and overwrought .

And Jeff. What would Laine have done without him? He'd

been more than a friend. Jeff had stood by her side, giving her support and strength.

During a rare moment, Laine had longed to lean on the God she knew as a child, but fear or confusion had blocked the road. She'd turned her back on the Lord years ago. How could she come to Him now with a heavy heart and expect His mercy?

With the last items boxed and packed in the truck, Laine gave a final look, locked the door, and slipped the key into her pocket. Proceeds from the sale of the house would become a small investment for Becca's future.

She looked up at Jeff. His eyes reflected his sorrow, and he wrapped an arm around her shoulder as she headed for the rented truck. Sliding onto the seat, she brushed the tears from her eyes and waited for him to start the engine. As he pulled away, she looked back one last time at Becca's past and then turned forward to face the future.

Sunday traffic was sparse, and soon Jeff was backing the trailer down her condo driveway. Knowing Mavis would bring Becca back in the middle of the afternoon, Laine and Jeff hurried the boxes into the basement. The child needed no added stress, seeing her mother's belongings packed away. Someday, when the time was right, Laine and Becca would share memories of Kathleen. The thought sent Laine's memory back to the day a week earlier—one of her last days with Kathleen—when the two sisters had reminisced about their childhoods. Becca couldn't spend time with her mother as she grew to be an adult, but Laine would share a wealth of her own memories with the orphaned girl.

"What do you think?" Jeff asked, setting the last screw into the shelving unit. "Becca should like all this storage."

"I want to get her books and some toys on them before she gets here." Laine felt her throat constrict with emotion. "Make it seem more like home. I hope bringing the furniture and bedding from her old room will make it seem more familiar."

Jeff braced his hand against an empty shelf. "You've done all you can, Laine. Every little thing helps."

"Nothing will help," she said, feeling her sorrow rise to the surface. A sob escaped, and tears rolled from her eyes.

In a heartbeat, Jeff reached her side, his arms drawing her close, his shoulder a sponge for her grief. Soothed by his quiet compassion, Laine pulled herself together, wiped the moisture from her face, and tucked back her shoulders. "Thank you. I'm glad I got that over with before Becca arrived."

"God gives you permission to cry, Laine. You and Becca. Tears are cleansing."

I don't want God's permission, Laine thought. *He took Kathleen's life and made Becca an orphan. I blame God. . . so why ask His approval?* Her bitterness fell like lead against her heart. Struggling, she pushed the hostility away. She recalled the verse her mother had so often quoted: *There is a time for everything and a season for every activity under heaven.* Laine shook her head. What purpose could a merciful God find for allowing this to happen?

"Okay," Jeff said, rubbing his hands together. "Let's get these shelves filled. It's almost three o'clock."

Surprised at the lateness of the hour, Laine let her thoughts shift to action. As she pulled books and knickknacks from the boxes, Jeff placed them on the shelves; and when they were finished, Laine added a few stuffed animals to the room and bed, then tossed the leftovers in Becca's toy chest bench and surveyed the room.

"What do you think?" she asked. "Presentable?" She jolted, hearing the door slam.

Jeff grabbed the last two boxes from the floor and carried them into the hallway.

"Toss them in my room," Laine said, rushing down the hallway toward the front door.

Reaching the kitchen, she found Becca standing by the table, clutching Penny in her arms and holding a duffel bag.

Laine opened her arms and knelt as Becca hurried toward her and pressed her head against Laine's shoulder.

"Did you have a nice visit?" Laine murmured, afraid to speak any louder lest her own sadness spill into her voice.

Mavis watched them from the doorway, then gave Laine a wave as she turned toward the driveway. The sound of her car's motor and the crunch of wheels on the gravel followed. When the sound faded, Laine pulled herself up. "Are you okay?"

Becca nodded. "Are you?" she asked with wisdom beyond her years.

"I'm okay. About like you," she said, wanting to be honest. "Jeff and I fixed your room, but you can move things around the way you like them."

"Where's Jeff?" she asked, her head turning toward the doorway.

"He's in the other room." She took Becca's hand. "Want to say hello?"

The child didn't answer but moved toward the hallway, and Laine stayed back, letting her pass through the doorway first.

Jeff's voice sailed down the hall. "Hi, Angel."

"What are you doing?" Becca asked, her voice carrying down the hall.

"I'm admiring your bedroom," he said, his tone filled with encouragement.

Laine waited a moment, letting Becca survey her new bedroom with Jeff before she headed down the corridor. When she reached the doorway, Jeff had Becca in his arms, and they were sorting through the top shelf.

He looked over his shoulder and grinned. "She likes the books in a special order."

"I like things in order too," Laine said, walking toward them and watching Becca shift the volumes on the shelf.

"I'm looking forward to reading some of your books."

"We can read them together," Becca said.

Laine sent her a smile. "Sure thing."

"And I like puzzles. Do you like jigsaw puzzles, Jeff?" Becca asked, squirming in his arms.

He lowered her to the floor. "Love 'em," he said, wagging his eyebrows at Laine.

Becca surveyed the room, then headed to the toy box. She dug inside and pulled out two puzzle boxes. "This one has kittens in the picture. See." She tilted the box for Jeff.

Jeff nodded. "Do you like kittens?"

She grinned. "Kittens and puppies. . .and puzzles. Will you help me?"

"Only if your aunt will cook us some food while we put them together." He folded his arms and eyed Laine.

"Right," Becca said, imitating Jeff's stance to perfection, "only if you make us dinner."

Laine's aching heart exploded with love. "I'd like to do nothing better."

Becca giggled as she piled the puzzles in her arms and headed through the doorway.

Jeff sent Laine a tender smile.

"Thank you," she said. The words sounded so simple in comparison to her depth of gratitude.

He nodded and hurried out the door to do Becca's bidding.

When she reached the kitchen, Laine opened the refrigerator and stared inside. What would Becca enjoy? Thinking of possibilities, she stepped into the living room but halted as she overheard their conversation from the porch.

"You know what?" Becca asked

"What, Angel?"

"I miss my mommy." Her voice wavered with loneliness.

"I know," Jeff said, "Just remember that. . ."

Unable to listen, Laine took a step back and fled to the

kitchen, her eyes brimming with tears. Pressing her knotted hands to her heart, Laine caught her breath and hugged the silence. With her life spinning like a top, she closed her eyes and whispered another thank-you, grateful for the handsome man who'd willingly joined her and Becca on the wild, whirling ride.

❧

Though the sunlight glinted through the window, Laine felt wrapped in gloom. Clearing the last of the breakfast dishes, she looked out to the screened porch. Like a tiny robot, Becca sat at a table with a box of crayons and a coloring book, her cheek resting against her left hand. Penny lay beside the crayon box, always close to her side.

Becca's emotions rolled like the tide. One minute, she acted like the happy child she'd always been, and the next, she bottled her emotions as tightly as she usually clutched the rag doll. Laine had no idea how to proceed. Jeff's influence proved invaluable. When he appeared, Becca's sadness often skittered out of sight like a shy kitten.

Mavis, too, stuck by Laine's side. She'd been Kathleen's longtime neighbor, a good Christian woman who'd often tended Becca when Kathleen went out. When Kathleen became ill, Mavis had become more than a baby-sitter. She'd become a caregiver. Now Laine could ask for no better friend than Mavis. The woman's greatest gift was her willingness to stay on to care for Becca.

When Laine first approached her about caring for Becca while she was at work, Mavis smiled. "I've watched Becca grow from an infant to a little lady. How could I say no? I love her as if she were my own." Laine felt overwhelmed by her kindness.

Laine had no knowledge of Kathleen's other friendships except for one lady who'd appeared at the funeral and later at the house. Becca called the woman Aunt Pat, and any concern

Laine had about the stranger melted under the warmth of her niece's familiarity with the woman. She had been a poor sister for years. Kathleen certainly had needed a friend and apparently had found one in Pat.

A motion caught Laine's eye, and she turned toward the doorway and spotted Jeff at the door.

"It's unlocked," Laine called, heading toward him.

He pulled the door open and stepped inside. "All that sun outside, and you two are stuck in here. How about a boat ride or a walk on the beach? Becca, I saw some pretty stones washed up this morning. I think they have diamonds in them."

Becca raised her head and looked at him. "Real diamonds?"

Jeff flashed her a bright smile. "Well, maybe not real ones, but they're sure pretty."

The child swivelled in her chair and faced him. "My momma had diamonds." She lowered her head as if surprised at her own memory. "She said they were for me."

Jeff gave Laine a curious look, then turned his attention back to Becca. "You're a lucky young lady."

"Uh-huh," she agreed with a nod. Pausing for a moment, she turned to Laine. "Where are my diamonds, Auntie?"

Laine's heart sank. "I'm not sure, Becca. Hopefully, we'll find them someday." She knew where they were: in a pawnshop, most likely, or with some stolen goods dealer—wherever Scott Darian had unloaded them. Anger sizzled in her chest.

Becca gazed back at Jeff. "We'll find them someday," she repeated.

"That's great," Jeff said. "But until then, let's go check out those rocks. Okay?"

"Okay. Can we go, Auntie?"

Laine's heart lifted. Jeff did wonders for her and Becca. "Don't know why not."

She tossed the dish towel in the sink and slipped on her sandals. Becca grabbed Penny and headed through the doorway.

When they reached the beach, Laine slipped the sandals from her feet and tossed them on the dock, and Becca did the same. Dragging their feet in the shallow water, Laine and Jeff walked along the sand with Becca bounding off in front of them. Periodically, the little girl reached down to grasp a stone, then darted back to show them her prize before slipping it into her pocket.

Suddenly Laine caught sight of Becca and let out a gasp. Darting forward, she grabbed poor Penny, who hung precariously close to the water. She tucked the doll under her arm with Becca's permission, and they continued on their way.

"You look pretty cute carrying your doll there, Lady," Jeff teased.

"If I had anything to say about it, I'd pitch this poor thing and get her another. But if I harmed Penny, I'd be in deep trouble. Becca always loved this pitiful thing, but since Kathleen. . .died, she won't go anywhere without it. I don't know what I'll do when school starts in September."

"Hopefully she'll be doing a little better by then. Kids are resilient."

"I hope so." Moments of silence hung between them, then she added, "I've been meaning to thank you so much for helping me with Kathleen's things. I hated to do everything so fast, but it seemed easier that way."

"No problem. I'm glad I could help. You've got a lot on your mind right now, I know, and Becca's going to need a lot of love."

"I love her with all my heart, but she needs more than that. She needs time and attention, and with my new job, I don't know what I'm going to do. Her dad's mother can give her every chance in the world that I can't."

"This is none of my business, but you know what I think. Love is the most important thing anyone can give her."

Laine knew he was right, yet how could she close her eyes

to the opportunities, college, travel, social position—all those things the Keary family had to offer? "I don't disagree with you, Jeff, but I'll have to do what I'm led to do."

They continued in silence with their only interruption being Becca's shouts of glee when she found another "diamond" rock. Soon the child's pockets were weighted with pieces of stone.

Laine and Jeff filled their own pockets with the debris gathered by Becca since Laine didn't want to stop her. This was the first time the child seemed like herself since the day her mother had died.

Eventually, the three turned back toward the condo, and as they neared the neat, red-brick dwellings, Laine saw a lone figure sitting on the edge of the dock. As they drew closer, she detected a woman's form, but Becca was the first to identify the visitor.

"Aunt Pat," the girl called, skipping along the sand.

"Hi, Kiddo."

As they approached, Pat rose and met them. "I hope you don't mind my dropping by. You said 'anytime,' so I took you at your word."

Laine had given that invitation in an attempt to be hospitable to Kathleen's friend, but she'd expected a telephone call first. "I see you found us without trouble," she responded.

"Yes, your directions were clear." Pat eyed Jeff. "I don't believe we've met."

"Jeff Rice," he said, extending his hand.

"Pat Sorrento." She gripped his fingers, her eyes riveted to his.

Jeff cleared his throat and extracted his hand. "Well, I suppose I'd better get home." He eyed Laine with a curious look. "See you later." Turning on his heel, Jeff headed home.

Pat watched him walk away. "I hope I didn't interrupt anything."

"No. We went for a walk along the beach." She gave a tiny head nod toward Becca. "A little distraction this morning. Becca's been holed up inside too long."

"Ah, yes. I'm sure things haven't been fun."

"Would you like to come in?" Laine offered, not really wanting the woman's company. Yet guilt rippled through her thoughts. Pat had probably been closer to Kathleen than Laine had been, and the woman needed time to heal too. Becca's enthusiasm clinched it. She needed contact with her mother's old friends.

Laine guided Pat into the condo, and though she indicated a seat on the porch, the woman followed her into the house.

"Nice place," she said, gazing around the room. "Great the way you have a view of the water from the living room and the kitchen."

"I like it. How about some iced tea or soda?" Laine deposited the rag doll on the table and opened the refrigerator.

"Iced tea would be great."

As Laine poured the tea, Pat leaned against the doorjamb. "I'm sure things have been difficult for you and Becca. Even though Kathleen was sick for a long time, she seemed to go so quickly—it was almost as shocking as when Alex went."

"I know," Laine said. She handed Pat the glass. "Let's sit on the porch. Did you know Alex well?" she asked, glancing over her shoulder.

"Not really." The woman followed behind her. "Kathleen and I became friends after the plane crash."

Laine sank into a wicker chair, gesturing for Pat to sit. Silence hung on the air. As Laine pondered what the woman wanted from her, Pat finally spoke.

"You finished cleaning out the apartment, huh? Everything's gone?"

Laine nodded. "All, but a few mementos." Then Laine recalled why the woman had come. "Ah, yes. You'd asked for a remembrance. I'm sorry I forgot. Most everything's packed in the basement. Did you have something special in mind?"

Pat thought for a moment. "Nothing particular. A trinket. Maybe a piece of costume jewelry. She had a pretty pin she wore occasionally. Green stones, if I remember correctly."

"I don't recall it." How could she? For years, they'd barely been in contact. "If you can wait a minute, I'll run down and see if I can find a couple of the jewelry boxes." Laine eyed the woman, hoping she'd decline.

"If it's not too much trouble, that'd be nice."

Laine released a noticeable sigh, but Pat ignored it. She left Kathleen's old friend chatting with Becca and traipsed down the basement stairs. Reading the box labels, she finally located the one that held the velvet-lined jewelry boxes. Nothing of value had appeared to be inside when she gave it a cursory glance while they were packing, but she lifted the two boxes and carried them up the stairs.

Pat and Becca were coloring a picture when Laine returned, and she set the boxes on a side table and waited. In a few moments, Pat returned to her chair, and together the two women opened the jewelry boxes and peered at the brooches and earrings inside. Pat studied the pieces, tossing them back into the box while Laine waited.

"See anything you'd like?"

"I thought maybe something would catch my eye. You know, a favorite of Kathleen's, but I'm not spotting anything."

"This is all I remember, Pat, unless there's one more box down there I didn't notice. Give me your telephone number, and if I find another box, I'll give you a call."

Pat fingered a small gold brooch inset with a blue stone. "No, that's silly of me. This is pretty, and it was Kathleen's. I'll just take this one, if you don't mind."

"No, not at all. Take two if you'd like."

Pat closed the lid on the box without giving another glance

at the other jewelry and then gazed down at the pin. "Thanks. This one is fine." She sighed as she rose. "I've taken enough of your time. Thanks, Laine." She turned to Becca. "Kiss Aunt Pat good-bye, Kiddo."

Becca jumped up and planted a kiss firmly on Pat's cheek.

Pat turned back to Laine. "I appreciate your kindness, but I'd better get."

Laine followed her guest out to the driveway, and as the woman drove off, Laine gazed after her, sensing something but not knowing what.

Later that afternoon, Becca wandered into the living room and leaned her cheek against Laine's arm. The child broke her heart. Feeling helpless and confused, Laine wrapped her arm around the girl. "You okay?"

Becca didn't answer. She lifted her lovely blue eyes to Laine's. "Is tomorrow Sunday?"

"It sure is. Why?"

"Will you take me to Sunday school?"

Her question caught Laine off guard. "Sunday school?"

She nodded. "Mama always took me. But when she was sick, I went with Mrs. Dexter."

Laine felt her chest tighten. She had no idea Kathleen had kept up her church attendance. "Did she drop you off?"

Grasping the nearby rag doll, Becca pulled it into her arms, hugging it against her chest. "No, she went to church. Sometimes she went to Sunday school for big people."

A sinking sensation hit Laine's stomach. Now what? She didn't know what churches were nearby. But how could she deprive her niece of this tradition when the little girl obviously needed some things in her unsettled life to remain constant? She'd check the Yellow Pages or maybe call Jeff. He'd lived in the neighborhood longer. Maybe he'd know of a nearby church.

Laine focused on the child, who gazed up at her with curious eyes and a look of expectation. "Sure you can go to Sunday school." She smiled encouragingly. "We'll go tomorrow."

Becca's face brightened, and Laine sat with her for a few moments before she made an excuse and scurried to the telephone, hoping Jeff was home. When he answered on the second ring, she breathed a relieved sigh.

"Church?" A lengthy pause hung on the line before he continued. "Sure, let's see. There's Bloomfield Community Church and Christ Church. They're nearby. And then up on Long Lake is the First Church of Farmington. What's your pleasure?"

"Did you ever go to any of them?" Laine wrinkled her nose, expecting a negative response.

"Actually, I have. Christ Church is friendly. They seem to have a lot of young families with kids. Probably a good Sunday-school program, if that's what you're looking for."

Laine nodded, surprised at his answer. "Well, Becca asked about Sunday school. . .and I promised."

"What about her own church?" Jeff suggested. "You could go there."

"It's quite a distance, and I'm afraid it might bring back sad memories. I guess I'll check out Christ Church tomorrow."

"If you'd like some company, I'll join you. Makes it easier if you have a friend."

"You would? You're kidding."

"No problem. Certainly can't hurt me." Amusement brightened his tone. "In fact, it might do me some good."

"But I thought you said you weren't a practicing Christian."

A chuckle came over the wire. "I don't have to 'practice.' I know how," he said. "I just don't."

She voiced a feeble "oh," not knowing how else to respond.

"I suppose you're wondering why I said I don't go to church, and now I'm telling you I go occasionally."

"I guess that's what was going through my mind."

"Once in awhile the urge hits me. . .like tomorrow. I have the urge to go with you."

"I'm glad," Laine said. "Thanks. I'll check the times and call you."

When she replaced the receiver, she stood for a long time staring at the telephone. The man seemed to meet every need she had. Strange but nice. She'd leaned on him during the tragedy of Kathleen's death, yet she barely knew him. Sometimes she felt as if God provided for her needs in the strangest ways. Goose bumps rose on her arms at the thought.

four

"Get up, Auntie," Becca called.

Laine opened one sleepy eye and gazed at the smiling child leaning against the bed, her chin propped against the pillow. The smiling part surprised her. She opened her arms to Becca, and the little girl climbed onto the bed and kissed her cheek.

"Time to get up, Auntie. You promised we'd go to Sunday school."

Laine's pleasant expression flattened. She'd do most anything for Becca, but this request wasn't easy. She hadn't been in church for years. She'd even arranged for Kathleen's funeral to be held in the chapel at the funeral home, rather than face an hour or two in church where guilt stabbed at her. But today she had little choice.

She swung her feet over the bed and sat next to Becca. "You're really going to make me get up out of this wonderful bed, aren't you?"

Disappointment edged Becca's face, and Laine felt sorry she'd said anything at all. "Did I tell you who's going with us?"

Becca swung her saucy dark brown curls back and forth in a dramatic "no."

"Jeff." Laine stood and put out her hand for Becca to join her. "So I think we'd better hurry and get ready before he comes."

Becca hurried off toward her room. Laine let a heavy sigh drain from her. She had to be more careful how she spoke to the child.

She showered quickly, and since Becca had bathed the

night before, the five year old was nearly dressed when Laine found her in her room. The little girl sat on her bed, talking to Penny.

Laine's thoughts darted around her promise to Kathleen, wanting what was best for her niece. She needed to make contact with Glynnis Keary. As the fraternal grandmother, Mrs. Keary had a right to know about Kathleen's death. Though they'd been estranged, Laine believed Becca's grandmother should have some input into Becca's future.

As the thought filled her mind, she wondered if her desire to talk to Becca's grandmother was based on a lingering hope that the elderly woman might insist on taking the child. As the reality of the idea jolted her, for the first time she resisted it. Could she really let Becca go away? Despite the child's sad and sudden arrival in her life, Laine adored her, and Becca was all the family she had left.

A knock signaled Jeff's arrival, and when Laine pulled open the door, she stood transfixed for a moment until her embarrassment forced her to close her mouth and invite him in. Dressed in a suit and tie, his stubble shaped to a short, neat beard, he rattled her emotions like a dune buggy on a bumpy back road.

"It came, I see," she said.

His face creased in question as he surveyed her face.

"Your beard," she said with a chuckle. "I see it arrived."

He grinned back. "I'm just giving it a try. Hair today, gone tomorrow." He grimaced playfully. "Sorry. I couldn't help myself."

"Doesn't look bad at all, really. Adds a little character."

"Hmm? Sounds a little like a backhanded compliment."

Her words hadn't come out as she meant them. He had too much character, but the beard protected her from his firm square jaw and distracted her from his full, soft lips. She didn't want to tell him that. "A compliment. I'd never in this world accuse you of not being a character."

Before he came up with a rebuttal, Becca wandered from her bedroom, ready to go.

"Look what we have here," Jeff said with an admiring gaze. "And who might this lovely young lady be? A princess?"

Becca giggled. "It's me."

"You?" He tickled her under the chin. "I guess I should have known. But you look bright and shiny in your Sunday-school clothes."

She looked down at her royal blue dress with the pink trim. "It's new. Aunt Laine bought it for me. . .for my mommy's funeral." She lowered her head, her voice fading.

Jeff clapped his hands together uncomfortably. "Well then, I suppose we'd better be going. Can't be late for church."

Laine grabbed her shoulder bag, relieved that he had moved them along and changed the subject. But with each step toward the door, she grew closer to another difficult moment. Church. Her chest tightened, causing her to feel breathless.

❧

Laine stepped from the car, hesitant and concerned. Becca's early morning enthusiasm had continued during the ride to church, but Laine hoped the child would not be disturbed by memories of her mother once they were inside. Facing the truth, Laine's own dread knifed through her. With apprehension, she waited for Jeff by the passenger door. When he rounded the car, she and Becca joined him, and the three-some approached the red brick building.

From the church's classic design, Laine assumed it had been constructed long ago. The rectangular shape, topped by a tall steeple, took Laine back in time, and she fought the nostalgia that swept over her.

Entering through the double doors, she stood in the foyer and held her breath. Rather than facing the curved sanctuary or center altar of modern structures, she viewed an old-fashioned church like the one in her youth. It featured a center aisle flanked by long wooden pews. Ahead of her, stained glass glinted with the morning light, its colors spread like paint on the soft gray carpet.

Laine concentrated on the carpeting rather than the image created by the colorful glass. She could not confront Jesus' anguished face spotted with blood from His crown of thorns or His outstretched arms offering her solace and mercy. She deserved no mercy.

A deep ache reached to every limb. She pushed away her memories in an attempt to soothe her wavering spirit and turned from the sanctuary. Looking at the foyer walls, she spied an arrow pointing toward the Sunday-school rooms. With Becca at her side, Laine took the stairs and located the woman in charge of new-student registration. When she'd completed the form, Laine followed along to the preschool class. She kissed Becca's check, and after promising to meet Becca when church was over, Laine forced herself back up the steps.

Jeff waited by the inner doors. He motioned her toward the sanctuary as the first hymn began. When they were seated, Laine longed to make an escape, but the weight of her sorrow nailed her to the hard wooden pew. Why could she not raise her head? With Kathleen's forgiveness, she should feel a sense of relief, a desire to move on. But her guilt clung to her like an insect in a spider's web.

A dark blue hymnbook stood in the rack, and Laine pulled it out, checked the song board, and thumbed through the pages. When the first verse began, the congregation rose, and she pulled herself up on quaking legs. Why had she allowed Becca to drag her here? She glanced at Jeff's calm profile, his pleasant voice singing the words to the familiar song. Apparently sensing her attention, he turned and smiled, his appearance comfortable and accepting.

The song of praise filled the room, and pulling her attention from the blurred words, Laine garnered courage and focused on the stained-glass windows. Not one image but many. Surrounding a lily-entwined cross, Laine viewed scene after scene of Jesus' miracles—healing a leper, turning water into wine, raising Lazarus, opening the eyes of the blind man.

Fighting her emotions, a sound reverberated through her mind—a voice as strong as thunder: *Laine, why do you wait to open your eyes? Why do you wait to be healed?*

❧

"How are those pancakes?" Jeff asked Becca as they dawdled over their after-church breakfast.

"Good." She turned her reticent blue eyes toward his.

What had made the difference? Jeff wondered. She'd clammed up after Sunday school. In fact, after they left church, Becca and Laine had become a silent twosome. Laine's discomfort had struck him as soon as they'd entered the building. Tension ticked in her jaw. Her lithe body looked rigid as if she were a soldier standing at attention. No smile, only dread filled her eyes. She'd mentioned one day that she'd drifted from her faith and needed to forgive herself, but her cryptic statement remained a secret. And he didn't have the right to ask.

Silence hung over the table, and he shuffled his feet, pushing back his dauntless curiosity until he lost the battle. "So, Becca, what did you think about Sunday school? Were the people nice?"

She moved her head up and down slowly, taking a sip of milk and wiping off the mustache it created. "They were nice."

"But it was different, huh?"

She nodded again. "I like my old Sunday school best. . . with my mom." Her eyes glistened with moisture.

Jeff swallowed back his own surprising emotion. He was tough. How could those two blue eyes wring such empathy from him? "You know what?"

Her head lifted, and she fixed her gaze on his.

"Change is hard for everyone, especially when it's sad." Jeff said. "And it's okay for you to feel very sad sometimes. I'm sad too, once in awhile. I'm sad when you are."

A look of interest rose on her face. "Did your mom die?"

"Yep, that was sad for me even though I'm a grown-up."

"When I get big, I just want to be happy."

Even Laine grinned at the child's statement.

"Well, I'll tell you what. I pray you get your wish." He turned his head to catch Laine's eye. Her face revealed a multitude of emotions—sadness, longing, amusement, pain. She slid her hand across Becca's shoulders, and the child looked up at her, wide-eyed, then relaxed. So did Laine. She shifted her gaze to Jeff. "Thanks for coming along with us this morning. And for suggesting breakfast."

"You can always count on me to think of food."

Amusement played on her lips. "The way to a man's heart."

"Among other things." His own cryptic message soared out before he harnessed it.

Laine tilted her head but didn't comment, and he felt relieved. These two ladies had carved a niche in his heart, a niche he'd never before allowed to occur. But he'd lost control. Like Laine's Superman, he wanted to rescue them from hurt and carry them away to a brighter day. But for now, that was impossible.

He eyed Becca coddling the rag doll. They'd convinced her to leave it in the car during church, but like a little mother, she insisted the raggedy thing join them for breakfast.

His gaze shifted from Becca to Laine. "So what exciting things do you have planned for this bright Sunday afternoon?" A shadow washed over Laine's face, and he was sorry he'd asked.

"I have a phone call to make—one I've been dreading."

"Oh?"

"To Becca's grandmother."

Becca's eyes shifted upward, listening intently.

"Have you talked to her at all since—?" Jeff lifted the coffee mug to his lips.

"No, but I must. I'd like to meet with her. I think we need to talk." She dropped her napkin on the table with a sigh. "But I dread it. I'm not sure what I want to say or do."

"Worried or confused?" Jeff asked, returning the mug to the table.

"Both, I suppose. I'd thought a lot of things. . . ." She paused, gazing down at Becca's curious stare. "But I'm thinking differently now."

Her gaze moved back to him and then to her niece, making it clear she couldn't be specific with the child's ears so tuned to the conversation. He watched as she reassuringly slid her arm around Becca's shoulders and caressed her cheek with a finger.

"It's probably best if you take your time. Let me know if you need anything, okay? If you want to see her today, I'll be happy to. . .have Becca as my guest for a couple of hours." He hoped he'd said the right thing. He assumed Laine would prefer to speak to Becca's grandmother alone.

"Thanks. Mavis would keep Becca too, I think."

"No need, though. Becca's one of my favorite girls."

The child lowered her head with a giggle, and her smile lifted his heart. Her delicate face looked too strained for someone so young.

"Thanks. I'll see what happens. I might lose my nerve today. Though I know the sooner the better."

"I'd say. The longer you wait, the more strain you'll put on your meeting." He wondered how much involvement Becca had had with her father's family. Apparently little. Then he wondered why. He sipped from his empty coffee cup, amused at his preoccupation. A carafe stood on the table, and he grasped the handle, holding it toward Laine.

"Just a warm-up, thanks," Laine said.

Jeff poured a measure into her cup, then filled his own. He sensed a larger story here than Laine had offered. Was it a secret or details she didn't want to burden him with? How could he help to lift the pressure from her lovely shoulders? He closed his eyes, knowing he had burdens and pressures of his own he couldn't share with her—secrets that made loving someone too difficult.

five

Laine sat outside the large red-brick colonial and stared at the well-manicured lawn, trimmed hedges, and pruned trees. The inside would be as immaculate. Wealth oozed from the mortar of the stately dwelling.

The telephone call had been disjointed and brusque. Glynnis Keary withheld an invitation until Laine admitted Kathleen had died. She'd hoped to tell her in person. The only sound was an intake of breath shivering through the otherwise silent phone line.

What did she want from this visit? Money? No. Sorrow? No. A home for Becca? She gazed again at the opulence. Though her heart said no, reality suggested otherwise. Would the child be better off with this elderly woman who could give her time, advantages, and, she hoped, love? Her head and heart wrestled for an answer.

Laine pulled the key from the ignition, gripped the handle, and pushed open the door. Her legs weakened as she approached the entrance on the neat brick walk. The bell chimed, and she held her breath.

When the front door opened, her heart came to a standstill. She'd expected a servant to answer, but instead a neatly coiffed woman wearing tasteful makeup faced her. They'd never met, and the image Laine had created in her mind shattered. Instead of the haughty and detached countenance she'd expected, a strained, sad face stared at her.

"Laine?" The older woman's voice was rich and full, like a

mezzo-soprano, yet the hint of vibrato revealed her advancing years.

"Yes," she said, extending her hand. "And you're Mrs. Keary."

The woman nodded in acknowledgment as she stepped back, allowing Laine entrance to the foyer. Mrs. Keary's simple, yet elegant shirtwaist dress of burgundy silk swished around her upper calves. Her low, dark pumps moved silently on the carpeted floor. Laine gazed at the wide staircase leading upward, and beside the wide arch, an ornate table, holding an array of fresh flowers, reflected in the gilt-framed mirror on the wall behind it.

"Please come in." The woman led the way, and Laine followed.

Glancing down at her simple cotton skirt and plain blouse, she felt underdressed in the woman's company. With the wave of her hand, Mrs. Keary indicated a seat, and Laine lowered herself into a brocade chair facing a pair of French doors.

"Thank you for seeing me, Mrs. Keary. I didn't want to tell you about Kathleen on the telephone, but—"

"I left you no choice," she said, seating herself in the chair across from Laine. "I'm sorry. I hadn't heard from Kathleen in nearly three years, and. . .well, I certainly wasn't prepared for your news."

"She'd been sick, off and on, for a long time. I wish she'd let you know."

"Yes, I wish she had. And Rebecca? She's with you?"

Laine nodded, studying the woman as she mentioned Becca's name. A sad tenderness washed across the woman's pale face, leaving Laine with a greater ache. "Kathleen made me promise to take her before she died. I questioned her wisdom. I work long hours, and I'm single. But Kath insisted."

A lengthy hesitation sent a wave of discomfort edging through Laine. She waited for a response, a comment, something, wondering if one would come.

"And what would you have preferred?" the elderly woman finally asked.

Laine drew in a deep breath of courage. "At first I thought Becca should be here. . .with you."

The woman leveled her with her eyes. "At first?"

"You have time, money, benefits you can give her that I can't. But. . .I love her with all my heart, and she needs me. And I need her." Laine's eyes ached from holding the other woman's gaze, and she looked down to her cold trembling hands tucked in her lap.

"Who needs whom the most, I wonder?"

She wasn't sure if Mrs. Keary expected an answer. And she didn't know if she could respond. "Mrs. Keary, I—"

"Glynnis, Laine. Please call me Glynnis. I imagine, under the circumstances, we'll be seeing each other relatively often, and the less formality the better."

Her comment jolted Laine, the meaning lost somewhere in her confused thoughts. "Thank you." She organized her words. "Does this mean that you'd like to spend time with Becca?"

"I'm her grandmother. And you're correct. Time and money, I have in abundance. But. . .I must decide what's best for the child and for me. I need to develop a relationship with her. She doesn't know me at all. She was less than a year old the last I saw her."

"Yes, I know. After Alex's death, Kathleen didn't make any effort to stay in touch with his family. But you didn't either, from what I understand." Her words were sharp but true, and they needed to be spoken.

"I can't deny that. We were desperately disappointed in

Alexander's choice for a wife. We'd expected much more. Though your sister was beautiful and sweet, she lacked—"

"Breeding, status, money. Rather shallow things, Glynnis. You never gave her a chance."

"We never gave each other a chance." Glynnis's sharp, blue eyes nailed Laine to the chair. "I realize I had the upper hand, but if she'd put forth an effort, we would have relented, you know. We loved Alexander. And we could have learned to accept Kathleen too. According to my son, she was a loving wife. Apparently, she made him happy."

Tears pressed behind Laine's eyes. "And he made her happy. He loved her dearly. I'm sorry you didn't see it. After his death, she was terribly alone. Lost, except for Becca. She didn't have anyone to comfort her or give her support." She lifted her eyes to the woman's eagle gaze. "I let her down too."

Empty space hung between them. They sat, immobile. The heaviness pressed on Laine's chest, aching, her breathing painful like pneumonia. She forced her gaze to remain locked with the other woman's. Each needed to face their selfish, loveless actions.

This time Glynnis averted her eyes first. "And then the con man stepped in." An unmistakable shudder rippled through her. "Everything Alexander worked for she lost to an evil, sweet-talking man."

"Yes, I think he took most everything. I haven't forgiven myself for allowing it to happen. I don't know what either of us could have done. Maybe something. But we weren't there, and Scott Derian was."

"And where is this man now? Do you know?"

"I have no idea. Kathleen did nothing about it. She was embarrassed and felt used. When I realized what had happened, I tried to convince her to tell the police. But she refused. She said he'd get caught someday, swindling some other lonely woman. I'm sure he will."

"We hope."

Laine edged her gaze upward. "I pray." The word "pray" had distanced itself from her vocabulary for a long time, but in the current situation, it seemed the only fitting word to use. She needed to pray that Scott Derian received just punishment for his crime, for hurting Kathleen, but most of all, for hurting Becca.

"I'd like to see her," Glynnis stated without fanfare.

"I'd hoped you'd say that," Laine replied. But now that she'd heard the words, she wanted to embrace the child, protect her, keep her safe. Could she give Becca to this reserved, prim woman? Jeff was right. Becca needed more than money and time. She needed love and laughter. Could she find that here in this rambling, luxuriant house? "I'll bring her for a visit."

"I'd like to see her alone. I'm afraid, without meaning to, your presence would influence our relationship."

☙

So much time had passed since Laine had prayed. But today, as she sat in the car next to her condo, she lifted a prayer. If God didn't want to bless her, He would surely have compassion for Becca. Laine needed guidance. Had she made a grave error contacting Glynnis? Even the thought of losing Becca made her feel helpless and alone.

When she turned off the motor and opened the door to the warmer outside air, Becca's laughter sailed across the grass. She tugged at Jeff's arm as he sat in his yard, shaded by a tall elm. But Laine's pulse missed a beat when she noticed a woman also sitting beneath the tree. As she eyed the situation, Becca spotted her and came running across the grass to her arms.

"Auntie," she called as she ran.

Laine engulfed the petite, delicate child, wanting to hold her forever. She looked again at the two adults in the shade of the tree. "Who's with Jeff?"

Becca tilted her head. "Aunt Pat. She came to see me."

"Ah," Laine said, trying to sound pleased, but a strand of apprehension slithered through her. With their hands clasped, she followed Becca across the lawn, planting a smile on her face. "Pat. What brings you here?"

Her first words, though spoken to Laine, were aimed toward Jeff. "I just wondered how you both were. . .and if you needed any help." She finally faced Laine. "I'd be happy to take Becca off your hands for a few hours. Or come to your place if you need me to stay with her sometime."

Laine tensed, not understanding why she experienced this strange reaction to Pat. "We're doing great, Pat, but thanks. Usually Mrs. Dexter sits, but today was rather spur of the moment and Jeff offered." Why did she feel it necessary to apologize or explain her business to this woman?

Pat shrugged. "Well, the offer stands."

Pat's focus drifted back to Jeff, and her gaze dragged across his broad chest to his trim waist, then up again. Laine's hands knotted, and she forced them to relax. She was acting like a jealous girlfriend. . .and she had no right to feel that way.

Jeff turned toward her, his eyes like aspen leaves turning autumn hued. "So how did you make out?"

She had no desire to talk about the situation in front of Pat. "Fine." Her tight-lipped response clearly let him know how she felt.

He understood and asked no more. "So how about an iced tea, Pat?"

The woman shook her head, obviously sensing something was amiss. "No, I'd better be on my way." She stood next to the chair a moment, then shifted toward Becca. "Okay, Kiddo, Aunt Pat has to get going. How about a kiss?"

Becca planted a quick kiss on her cheek, and with a wave, the woman strode toward the street where she'd left her car.

Embarrassment crept up Laine's neck. She had blatantly shown her jealousy toward the woman. She hoped Jeff hadn't noticed. Sinking into the vacated chair, she stared at the sun-drenched water. "So what was that all about?"

"Well now," Jeff said, "you tell me."

"What do you mean?" She squirmed under his gaze.

"Do I really have to tell you? You don't like her, and I'm not sure what bothers you." He tilted his head, waiting for her to respond.

"I don't know either." She checked Becca to make sure she wasn't within hearing distance. "She makes me nervous. Like she has an agenda that I'm not sure about."

"Agenda?"

"I'm not talking about you either, Jeff. Some other agenda. I know I'm talking in riddles, but I sense something."

Jeff chuckled under his breath. "I understand." His gaze also drifted toward Becca and then back. "Tell me how you made out with the grandmother?"

Laine sighed, a long, unsteady breath, and told him about the encounter and her latest fears.

"I don't want to pry, but what's this all about? Why doesn't she know Becca? Obviously, Kathleen and she held bad feelings, but what happened?"

Laine laid the story out for him. She needed to talk, and he offered a willing ear. Most importantly, she needed someone with understanding and wisdom to help her weigh her decision.

Jeff rested his elbows on his knees, hands folded in front of him. "You mean they never relented. Even after Becca was born, no one gave in."

"She was only a few months old when Alex died. Maybe in time they might have, but. . ."

He waited while she sorted through her options for the right words.

"But Kathleen got involved with a man. Too soon, really. About a year after Alex died." The tears she'd kept under control sought release and rimmed her eyes. "I wasn't there when she needed me. No one was. Kathleen was totally alone with a new baby. She turned to Scott Derian."

He nodded as if he understood. "And where's Scott Derian now?"

"He split."

"Split? You mean he dated her for awhile, then walked out on her too?"

"Worse than that. He used her. Alex left her with a tidy sum of money. Scott was a con man, I guess. He wheedled his way into her life and walked out with most of her money and jewels."

Jeff tensed as his gaze locked with hers. "Money and jewels? What was his name?" He slid to the edge of his seat.

"Scott Darian."

"You don't have any idea where he is now?" Jeff asked, his eyes searching hers. "Did you suspect what he was doing?"

"I'd never met him, but from what Kathleen told me, I didn't like him at all. He seemed too slick and sleazy for me. His presence gave me an additional excuse not to see Kathleen."

Jeff leaned forward. "And your sister never reported this to the police?"

"She thought he loved her. . .and maybe she was embarrassed.

After he split, I told her to call the police, but she refused."

"Refused?" Jeff caved into the back of his chair, letting a burst of air escape his lungs.

"What? Why are you so upset?"

Jeff corrected his posture and relaxed. "I'm sorry. I can't bear men who prey on woman. It happened in my own family, and it doesn't set well with me, that's all."

"Really? In your family?"

He closed his eyes, and she could barely hear his response. "My mother."

"Your mother? You're kidding."

He flashed a fiery look her way.

"I'm sorry, Jeff. Obviously you wouldn't kid about that." She sighed. Her energy had been sapped away with so much happening—Glynnis, Pat, the retelling of her story, and then Jeff's statement. Too much.

She saw the pain in his face and couldn't ask him anything else.

&

In the middle of the next week, Laine came home from work with a thudding headache. All day she'd thought about Becca's visit with Glynnis. She'd agreed to drop her off for her first visit on Saturday, and though she knew the child should get to know her grandmother, fear filled her. What would she do if Glynnis wanted Becca? She had to decide what was best for the child and not what was best for her own needs.

Massaging her temples, she opened the garage entrance of the condo. She heard Mavis working in the kitchen and Becca talking to her at breakneck speed.

When Laine entered, the woman swung around as if she were jerked on a chain. Her face paled, and her hand rested against her chest. "Oh, it's you." Relief sounded in her voice.

"Is something wrong?" Laine asked, wandering deeper into the kitchen and laying her handbag and attaché case on the counter.

Mavis's eyes shifted to Becca, then back to her. "No, I didn't hear the garage door open. That's all."

Something more than that had caused her ashen face, but Laine understood her comment. Becca was within hearing distance. "Is that for dinner?" She noted the bowl of greens the woman had rinsed and placed in a wooden bowl.

"Yes, I have chicken breasts marinating in the fridge, and I thought you might enjoy a salad. It's such a hot day."

"Thanks so much. How many breasts?"

"There's extra. Four or five, I think."

Laine nodded and eyed Becca. She needed the child out of earshot. "Becca, would you go out to the front and see if Jeff's car is in the drive? Or maybe he's in the yard."

"Can he have dinner with us?"

"Maybe. If he'd like to."

The child slid off the chair, leaving her coloring book behind, and headed toward the front.

"What's wrong?" Laine asked. "Something's frightened you."

"Oh, I'm probably being foolish. I noticed a car drive up and down the street a few times. It slowed each time it passed, and once Becca was in the back. I called her, and when I did, the car sped away."

"Did you get a look at the driver?"

"No, he had a baseball cap pulled down low on his forehead. And my old eyes aren't what they used to be. He was too far away."

"You're sure it was a man?" Pat came to mind. She couldn't

help herself. The woman made her nervous.

"I saw the cap," the older woman said. "I suppose I assumed it was a man. Probably someone looking for an address, and I got myself all jumpy."

"Probably. But I appreciate you being watchful of Becca."

She nodded, her eyes focused on the salad fixings.

The front screen slammed, and Becca's pattering footsteps bounded through the living room. "He's coming," she called.

The words no sooner left her mouth then a knock sounded from the doorway. Laine leaned toward the front window that looked toward the water. "Come in, Jeff." Threading her way around the table and Becca, she stepped out to the screened porch. "Hi."

Jeff grinned, looking comfortable in cotton slacks and a sport shirt. "What's up?" he asked.

His smile, as always, wrapped her emotions like a soft blanket. She glanced into the kitchen through the porch window to make sure Becca was preoccupied. "Thought you might like some dinner. Grilled chicken and salad."

"Sounds great. And I just picked up some cookies at the bakery. Could be dessert."

"I think we have some ice cream too."

His perception was keen, and a questioning look stole over his face. "So what else is up?"

She glanced again toward the window. "I might need a listening ear again, if you know of one."

"No problem. I know two good ones." His eyes crinkled, and he winked. "And very willing ones."

"Thanks. But after someone goes to bed." She tilted her head toward the inside. "Dinner's in an hour, okay?"

"Sure thing. I'll get home and slip into some shorts. See you in a bit."

Jeff meant every word, and following dinner and spending an hour amusing Becca before her bedtime, he became Laine's listener. With the back door locked and bolted, they wandered outside, and sitting on the dock's edge, they dragged their feet against an occasional wave as they talked.

Laine opened her heart about Becca, her feelings and fears, and once those words settled on the quiet evening, she told him of Mavis's concern. "Like she said, the person may have been looking for an address, but I'm getting a little suspicious."

"It's always good to be careful. Did she get a license number? Or a description of the car?"

"She didn't say. She thought the driver was a man. He had a baseball cap pulled low on his forehead. I was thinking maybe a woman could easily hide under a cap."

"Any particular woman in mind?"

She raised her head at half speed and gazed into his teasing eyes. "Okay, so I've already admitted Pat makes me nervous. I don't know why."

"Look, maybe I can check her out." He paused. "At least I can try." He stared down at his hands folded in his lap.

"How can you check her out? Who do you know?"

"I have friends. I know a guy who might be able to find out something. Don't be so nosy," he said, grinning at her. "You know I work with computers."

She eyed him, wondering if he was planning to do something illegal. "You mean you have secret ways to get into records and things?" Her hand gripped the edge of the dock.

He unfolded his fingers and caressed the tension of her hand clamped to the dock. "There are ways to find out lots of things on computers, if you know how. That's the only secret."

"Illegal?"

"Would I do something illegal?"

His smile sent her pulse racing. "Maybe. But I'd like to think you wouldn't."

"Then think I wouldn't." He shifted her shoulders around toward the lake. "Instead, take a look at that sky." He pulled her back against him and supported her with his chest.

She gazed above the tree line, and a sigh stole from her lips. The blue horizon shimmered with a soft lilac glow. Filaments of orange and amber wove through the periwinkle backdrop like spun threads, and a velvety cloud lay in a pool of liquid gold. Within seconds the panorama melted to misty violet, deepening to magenta and plum, and a sliver of an early moon, like a slice of melon, slid from behind the cloud.

Jeff's even breathing faltered, and he slid his hand over her shoulder and feathered her cheek with his finger. "Quite a show, huh?"

As she turned to face him, their gazes locked, and she saw the blaze of swirling colors of his hazel eyes. His focus slid to her lips, and like a bee hovering on the edge of a flower, he lowered his mouth to hers in a warm, sweet, unexpected kiss. He drew back, seeking her approval, before he found her lips again, this time lingering longer and sweeter than before. A tremor of pleasure shimmered through her core.

He lifted his hand and tilted her chin. Gazing at her, he studied her face. "I've wanted to do that for a long time. And my imagination wasn't anywhere near as wonderful as reality."

For a pulse beat, her muffled voice hesitated. "You've taken my breath away." Her words were reality too. He'd thrilled her with his unexpected, gentle affection.

They sat for a moment longer before Laine rose on quivering legs and suggested they return to the house. Though Becca was safe inside, a lingering fear hovered in her mind. With Jeff's hand wrapped around hers, they ambled up the path to the house.

six

On Saturday, Laine reviewed for the twentieth time where they were going and why, but the explanation was more for herself since Becca seemed to understand already. Shortly after lunch, they climbed into the car, and Laine drove the few miles to the Keary residence.

When they pulled into the driveway, Becca stared at the large, impressive structure. "Is this a castle?" Her head tilted as she peeked under the windshield's upper frame to see the three-story colonial rise in front of her.

Laine's hands felt icy against the steering wheel, though the warm sun beating through the glass was barely cooled by the air-conditioning. "This is your grandmother's house, Becca."

"It's a big, big house," Becca said, grabbing the canvas bag filled with books and small toys. She looked toward Laine, her small fingers clamped on the door handle.

With her nod of approval, Becca flung the door open and slid out into the hot summer air. Laine followed. No way would she send Becca to the door without leaving the youngster with a final kiss.

After pushing the bell, they waited. Again, Glynnis opened the door herself and stood transfixed, gazing down at Becca, who stared back at the stranger who was her grandmother. The woman was again covered in a soft, silky dress, this time a deep-hued paisley print. Her gray hair lay in short, soft waves around her pale face—the only color, her penetrating, midnight blue eyes.

She opened the screen door and stepped aside. Becca

looked at Laine for approval to enter. She nodded, and the child stepped into the foyer.

"Don't forget my kiss, Becca." A strange peal of fear, perhaps panic, lifted in Laine's voice, and she cleared her throat to cover the emotion. She lowered herself to the child's level for the kiss.

As Becca turned, Glynnis halted them. "Please come in, Laine. We can have some tea before you leave. Let Rebecca have a moment to get to know me."

Laine closed her eyes, thankful for the older woman's thoughtfulness, and followed them into the elegant foyer.

Becca stood in the middle of the room, pivoting like a ballerina on a music box, as she gazed at the winding staircase and the crystal chandelier that sparkled high above her head.

A look of amusement washed over Glynnis's face, then she placed her ringed hand on Becca's shoulder to halt her turning. "Rebecca, you don't remember me. I'm your father's mother, Glynnis Keary."

Becca's mouth drooped, and her eyes lifted to the full-voiced woman, looking down on her. "Are you my grandmother?"

"Yes, I am your grandmother. Is that what you would like to call me? 'Grandmother?' "

Becca's gaze flew to Laine's and then, as quickly, returned to Glynnis. "Grandma," she said with certainty. "I'll call you Grandma."

"All right." Glynnis's face colored to a soft pink, but she accepted the child's decision.

Laine stifled a grin. Glynnis and "grandma" didn't make a good match, but she was pleased the woman hadn't tried to stop Becca from using the less formal title.

"Let's sit in here." Glynnis gestured toward the living room, and Becca followed behind her, lugging her canvas bag. Laine stayed behind, observing the situation.

Glynnis pointed to the same chair she had offered during the previous visit, and Laine sank into the seat. Becca backed up and leaned against her, showing a new shyness.

"Becca, show your grandmother the toys and books you brought from home. She'd like to see what you have in the bag."

The little girl stepped forward, tripping over the edge of the cumbersome sack, and emptied the contents onto the floor. Glynnis controlled what appeared to be a grimace.

Becca shuffled through the items, then handed her grandmother a torn page from the coloring book. "I colored this picture for you. You can put it on the refrigerator and see it when you cook dinner."

Glynnis accepted the jagged page, giving it due attention. "This is lovely, Rebecca. Thank you. I'll certainly find a nice place to keep it."

Laine chuckled to herself, knowing the housekeeper might enjoy the refrigerator location, but Glynnis would probably never see the picture there.

As the child dug for a book from her pile of belongings, the housekeeper entered the room with a tray. She stepped around Becca and slid tea things onto the low table. She turned and left as quietly as she'd entered.

After pulling a book from the hill of toys, Becca slid it into Glynnis's hands. The child stood beside the chair as her grandmother flipped through the pages. "I'll read this with you later. Would that be all right?"

The child agreed.

"Would you like some milk and cookies, Rebecca?"

A hint of a smile rose on Becca's lips, and she sat on the floor and scooted up to the low table. Penny appeared from the pile of toys, and she sat the raggedy doll in her lap as she waited.

Glynnis stopped, the cookie plate suspended in air, and gazed down at the doll. "Oh my, Rebecca, do you still have that old doll? That's the first present your father bought for you. I remember when he showed it to me. I thought of all the lovely dolls in the world, why did he buy you a rag doll?"

"She loves it," Laine offered. "She takes it with her everywhere."

Glynnis blinked her eyes as if awaking and turned to Laine. "She does? I am surprised."

"The doll means a lot to her. Memories, maybe."

"Yes, perhaps that's it." Pulling herself from the nostalgic moment, Glynnis sat the glass of milk on the table nearest Becca and offered her cookies on a napkin.

Laine accepted her cup of tea. With her hand trembling faintly, she moved the cup to her lips, then breathed a deep, cleansing breath, hoping to relax.

While the goodies distracted Becca, Glynnis turned to Laine. "I've been wondering if anything is left from Alexander's estate. Money or the gems? The whole situation breaks my heart. At least I would like Rebecca to have something from her father's inheritance."

Laine lowered her head, not wanting to be the one to disappoint the woman. Her voice caught in her throat, and she swallowed the hard knot that pressed against her vocal cords. "A small amount of savings was left. I'm the beneficiary, but naturally the money is Becca's. Nothing else that I've found."

"Nothing? The emeralds that had belonged to my mother? The diamonds?"

At the word, Becca turned to her grandmother. "My mommy had diamonds for me. Where are they, Auntie Laine?"

Laine squirmed with discomfort. "We haven't found them yet, but we'll keep looking." She looked helplessly at Glynnis.

"Yes, do keep looking. The diamonds were priceless. And the emeralds. . .were my mother's." Her words faded to a sorrowful murmur.

A sinking sensation slithered through Laine's body. What could she do? She had no idea what Scott Derian did with the gems. How could she ever find them?

࣌

As she pulled into the condo driveway, Laine hit the garage door opener and parked the car. Since hearing the disturbing news of the strange car that week, she'd bolted the front and back doors before leaving. The only easy access to the house was from inside the locked garage. Anxiety was an uncomfortable emotion, and like a new sliver, its presence was felt every moment.

Glynnis offered to bring Becca home later in the evening, so Laine headed for her bedroom and slid into a pair of shorts and tank top. Sun and air might revive her and relax her tensed nerves.

She stopped in the kitchen and filled a tall glass with ice cubes, then poured herself some bracing tea. Returning the pitcher to the refrigerator, she glanced at its contents, knowing she'd eat dinner alone. Her stomach knotted in confusion, and she closed the door. Right now, food was her last concern.

Carrying her drink, she unbolted the door and stepped onto the porch. The midafternoon sun had ducked behind a cloud, and a refreshing breeze wafted through the open jalousie windows. She grabbed a canvas chair and reached to unhook the screen door. Her breath slammed against her heart as she stared at the hook and attached eye hanging from the doorjamb. Someone had forced the door open.

She dropped the chair and set her glass on the narrow sill. Swinging around, she eyed the front door. A gouge in the wood jarred her. Someone had tried to force open the door, but the deadbolt had discouraged them. Yet the two windows were intact. Why had they stopped at the door? To avoid the noise of breaking glass? Or had someone scared them away?

Her heart pulsed wildly. Had she perhaps halted the break-in? Did the sound of her car pulling into the garage frighten someone away? Her legs quivered beneath her, and she sank to the nearest chair. She needed to look around, but first she had to get a grip on herself. Why had this happened? What did someone want? The question seemed foolish. She knew the answer. Something of Kathleen's—it had to be. The whole mess began after she moved Kath's stuff to the condo.

But what? She'd gone through everything. Her sister had nothing left. One thing was certain: Someone else didn't know that. She leaned forward against the screen, looking toward Jeff's. Was he home? She'd rather he be with her when she looked around the house. Just in case.

She rose, her legs still jellylike, and went to the telephone. After four rings, the machine answered, and she left a simple message, "Could I see you when you have a minute?"

Her thoughts of relaxation marched away through the damaged door. Instead, she sipped the tea and waited. Questions shuffled through her mind. Scott Derian had split. If he'd hoped for more from Kathleen, why did he leave so abruptly? Staying by her side, he could have swindled the rest of her inheritance. Unless something happened. Had Kathleen become suspicious? Had she confronted him about how he handled her money?

From what Laine knew, Scott had supposedly advised her on investments. She entrusted her inheritance to him, bit by bit. He presented her with monthly investment reports. All bogus, she had learned after he vanished.

Laine closed her eyes, a deep, aching nausea rising within her. If she'd only been there to see what was happening. Love could blind a trusting person. And Kathleen had loved him— or maybe had needed a friend. Whatever, she'd trusted Scott.

"Hi."

Laine jumped at the sound. Jeff paused outside the door, his approach so silent she hadn't heard him.

"Thanks for coming over," she said, rising. "Open the screen and look at the hook and eye."

As he swung the door open, his gaze lit upon the door-jamb, and he paused. "What? Someone tried to break in?" His brow furrowed deeply as his eyes sought hers.

She nodded. "That's the only thing I can imagine. I took Becca over to her grandmother's earlier. I was gone maybe an hour. Hour and a half at most. It was like this when I got back."

"Anything missing?"

She shrugged. "I waited for you. Too afraid to look on my own. But I don't think he got in. See the front door. Either he gave up or was interrupted. He could've easily broken in through the windows."

Jeff studied the gouges in the wood, then wandered from one window to another. "How about the other doors and windows? You didn't check?"

"No, but I suppose we should." She turned and led him through the outside door. They circled the house, finding nothing disturbed. No prints in the earth beneath the windows. Next they returned to the house and searched through each room. Nothing. Whoever had tried to get in had failed.

Laine faced him. "This has to be connected with Kathleen. I've wracked my brain, and that's all I can imagine." She told him the thoughts that had gone through her as she'd waited for him to come home. "Does that make sense?"

"As much sense as anything. But you're telling this to the wrong person, you know."

"What do you mean?"

"The police, Laine. You need to call the police and report this."

"But nothing happened. He didn't get in."

"Do you want to wait until he does? Call them. Don't be foolish. That's what they're there for."

"Will you wait with me?"

He glanced back toward his house. "I have some things I need to do." He put his arm around her shoulder. "You can do that by yourself, can't you? Just call the number and tell them what happened. They'll send a car out. No problem."

Disappointment edged through her. Jeff always seemed to be around to offer support, but she was an adult. And she certainly didn't want to be another Kathleen. She'd criticized her sister for not reporting her situation to the police. She gazed at Jeff with a beseeching gaze, but he only chuckled.

"Listen, when's Becca due home?"

She shrugged, having only a vague idea. "Sometime this evening, after dinner."

"Well then, here's the deal. You handle the call, and I'll go over and come up with something for our dinner. How's that?"

"Suppose that's better than you holding my hand for a phone call."

"I knew you could do it."

"You've spoiled me, that's all. Whenever I need you, I find you nearby. Thanks for checking the place out with me."

"No problem. And when the police finish, come over. I'll be fixing you something wonderful for dinner."

He gave her a wink and hurried through the door. She watched him cross the lawn, pleased he'd thought about dinner plans, yet wishing he'd stick around while she dealt with the police.

seven

After dinner at Jeff's, Laine sat alone on her porch and listened for the car bringing Becca home. While she waited, the events of the past few hours dragged through her mind. The police had arrived quickly, checked the house just as she and Jeff had done, then jotted down a report and asked a few questions.

Finally, she did what should have been done long ago. She told her sister's story. Though the version was brief, she related everything. She noticed sidelong glances when she got to Scott Derian's role. Obviously, they'd heard similar stories.

Leaning her head against the wicker love seat, her thoughts drifted back to Jeff. Once again his cooking surprised her, grilled salmon fillets with herbs and bread crumbs, a salad, and fresh raspberries on vanilla ice cream. She closed her eyes, reliving his arm pulling her to his side and his kiss as tender as the last.

He seemed so different from other men she'd dated. They'd pressured and connived for more than kisses, but she'd always stood her ground. Their scheming turned her off—not on—and had pushed her right out of the dating scene for awhile. Laine was tired of the wrestling match.

Though her faith had taken a shaky turn, her Christian morals and upbringing had apparently carved a deep set of values in her heart. As the faintest desire rose in her mind, an image of Jesus rose even brighter, then her mother's watchful eyes filled her heart. So her suitors left her side disappointed.

To her surprise, temptation had taken a new twist after meeting Jeff. He seemed to follow her same moral beliefs. Yet never before had she fought such a fierce battle against her own passions. But Jesus, like her guide and shield, lifted in her mind, and her struggle faded.

A noise sounded outside, and her heart raced with anxiety. Becca's excited voice drifted through the open window, and she relaxed. No burglar. And Becca had weathered her first visit with her grandmother successfully. At least so it seemed from the sound of her exuberant voice.

Laine met her at the door. Glynnis stood outside the car with watchful eyes. Becca, dragging a bulkier canvas bag than when she'd left that morning, took Laine's hand.

"You had a nice visit?" Laine asked the child, already knowing the answer.

She nodded. "Grandma bought me a new doll."

Laine's heart gave a tug. Poor Glynnis didn't understand. A new doll would sit in Becca's room. Nothing replaced Penny. She released Becca's hand and stepped toward the automobile. "I see Becca had a wonderful time," she said, approaching the woman.

"Yes, we both enjoyed the day. She's a lovely child. Kathleen did a good job raising her." She lowered her eyes for a heartbeat. "I wish I'd been able to tell your sister."

"I wish you had too. But wishes are just that. So. . .what do you have in mind as far as Becca is concerned?"

"Perhaps an overnight stay. Rebecca seems willing. I did mention it to her."

Laine's stomach quivered like an aspen leaf. "If Becca is willing, I have no problem." Her heart thudded to her toes with her lie. She had a problem, but the concern was selfish and hers alone.

Glynnis returned to the car, and as the headlights faded, Laine returned to the house, planting a smile on her face for Becca.

ða

Sunday morning, the alarm rang, waking Laine and making her want to bury herself under her covers. But Becca's gentle reminder of Sunday school had arrived as she'd tucked the little girl into bed the night before. Laine was sorely tempted to turn off the alarm, roll over, and forget about her promise, but duty nudged her. Forcing her legs over the edge of the bed, she rose and dressed.

Less than an hour later, as they neared the church building, Laine initiated her plan. "I have some things I need to do this morning, Becca, so I'll drop you off at Sunday school and meet you outside right after, okay?"

As she slid Penny onto her lap, Becca lifted her eyes to her. "You aren't going with me?"

"Well. . .I thought you wouldn't mind." Her voice faded as disappointment settled on the child's face. "But if you really want me to, I'll stay with you."

Becca ran her hand over Penny, patting the pitiful looking doll. "Mommy went with me. Sometimes she stayed in Sunday school for big people, and sometimes she went up for church. You could go to the grown-ups' class."

A deep sadness rolled through Laine's chest, and tears she'd nearly conquered rammed against the back of her eyes. "I'll do that, Becca." She drew her hand down Becca's arm, resting it on her small fingers clutching Penny's cloth body. "I won't leave you, Sweetheart."

The child's tensed shoulders eased against the seat back, and they rode on in silence, each in her own thoughts.

At the church, they headed for the Sunday-school rooms.

Laine's dawdling left them with little time to spare. The church service had already begun, and the organ's deep pipes sent faint vibrations along the oak floorboards.

The classroom hummed with children wriggling in nearly every seat, and Laine's feelings tugged at her, eyeing the teacher who had to handle the overrun of active students. The woman smiled as she entered and pointed to an empty chair near the front.

Becca hesitated, peering at all the faces turned to her. Laine pushed her forward down the zigzag row of chairs, then backed away as the girl took her seat. But Laine's own retreat was not made quickly enough.

"Excuse me," the teacher said, edging around a child and approaching her. "Are you headed to the service? Or could I prevail on your kindness?"

Laine's eyes widened as she sensed the woman's problem, and she squinted, then plastered a pleasant expression onto her tensing face. "You need something?" Her question was ridiculous. Obviously the woman needed help, but Laine decided to play dumb.

"Well. . .I wondered if. . .the girl who usually helps me left a message that she's ill this morning, and as you can see, I have quite a group here. I could use some help. . . ." Her eyes lifted to Laine's. "Especially during the activity after the story."

Her request reflected in her wide, blue eyes, and Laine couldn't say no.

The woman's shoulders relaxed with a sigh. "I'm Sue Barker, by the way. And your daughter is so pretty. I thought so when she came last week."

"Thanks, but she's my niece. Her mother passed away recently, and she's living with me." She offered her hand. "I'm Laine Sibley."

Sue's face reflected her shifting emotions. "Oh, I'm so sorry." Her gaze darted toward Becca. "Thanks for helping out."

She pointed to a chair, and Laine worked her way around the throng of children and tucked herself into the space and folded her hands. Looking around the room at the eager faces, she ended her inspection on her niece. Becca's eyes glowed.

Laine grinned and leaned back, washed by nostalgia when she saw the woman's teaching material. An easel standing to the side held a large surface covered with black velvet. Flannel graph. How many years had it been since Laine had heard a Bible story told on flannel graph?

Animated and collected, Sue faced the children. "Today we're going to hear a wonderful story about forgiveness. Now who can tell me what forgiveness is?"

Laine watched as hands flew in the air. Four- and five-year-old children defined a word she'd struggled with for too long. The time flew as Sue marched the cloth figures through the story of the paralyzed man who walked away after Jesus' forgiveness. Her own heart leaped and tugged at the message.

When the story ended, each child received a paper bearing the picture of a heart with the word "forgiveness" arching inside its shape. The youngsters took the red magic markers provided and colored—some neatly and some with wild abandon.

Laine helped clean the red from their eager hands and, with round-ended scissors, guided some and cut for others the heart-shaped pictures. With small safety pins, they attached the red hearts to each child's top. Sue offered one to Laine and pinned another on herself.

The lesson ended with the children singing an a cappella rendition of "Jesus Loves Me" as they placed their hands over their hearts. Laine joined them, but beneath the paper adornment, her heart tumbled and throbbed with the story of the forgiven man and her own need for forgiveness.

❧

Sunday afternoon, Jeff wandered outside, wondering where Laine had been all day. Becca sat in the grass and called to him. "Aunt Laine's my new Sunday-school teacher."

"Is that right?" Jeff stammered, amazement barreling through him. "That's nice." He felt sure there was more to Becca's statement. Looking for Laine, he swivelled his head toward the enclosed porch.

Laine appeared at the window screen. "Not quite right. I gave the teacher a hand today since her assistant was sick." She turned toward her niece. "Now don't get your hopes up, Becca. That was only for today."

Sitting on the grass, Becca lifted her gaze to Laine. "But you could be, Auntie. She would let you come every week."

"I'm sure she would. But I'm not making any promises. And you can forget that hangdog look of yours too."

Becca looked at Jeff. "What's a hangdog?"

He ran his hand across his mouth, playfully wiping away his grin. "She's teasing, Becca. Hangdogs aren't really anything."

"Oh," Becca said with a smile. "Hangdog sounds funny."

"It does." He flashed a secret smile toward Laine. "And what did you and your auntie learn in Sunday school?"

Laine peered at him through the screen and muttered, "Don't push your luck."

Becca looked up to the sky, ignoring Laine's comment, and thought for a moment. "I learned about a man who couldn't walk, and people put him through a hole in the roof to see Jesus." She paused, her eyes squinting in concentration. "When it rained, did the people get wet with the hole in their roof?"

Laine opened her mouth to explain, but the thrust of the story took hold, and the child continued.

"And Jesus was so happy that the man wanted to see Him, He forgave his sins."

"Wow! That's a good story, so what did—"

"But wait, there's more," Becca said, her hand on her hip. "The man who couldn't walk stood up and carried his bed away when Jesus forgave him."

Jeff staggered backward. "Wow! That's even better. So what did that story teach you?"

Becca scowled and lowered her eyes, then a bright smile lit her face. "When Jesus makes you better, He makes everything better."

"That's a pretty important lesson for all of us, I think," Jeff said, nodding slowly and grasping his bearded chin. He sidled a glance toward Laine. She had mentioned drifting from church and needing forgiveness. He hoped the lesson had made an impact.

He faltered, remembering how he needed to deal with forgiveness issues too. For so long he'd lived with revenge motivating his life, wanting to get even for his mother's humiliation and loss from a con man like the man who had exploited Kathleen. Like the paralyzed man from Becca's Bible story, his life was handicapped by the driving force of vengeance. If Jesus forgave him his sin, maybe he could walk again without feeling the burden he'd carried for so long. He. . .and Laine too.

"Step on your tongue?" Laine asked.

He lifted his eyes as Laine strolled from the porch.

"You got pretty quiet there, Mr. 'Not Very Subtle.' "

"Sorry. Guess I was thinking of my own situation. I have no room to judge anyone. I have my own problems."

She sauntered his way, but the expression on her face told him she'd been thinking about the lesson. And hearing Becca's simple words was definitely something to focus on. When Jesus makes you better, He makes everything better.

eight

During the week, Laine thought about the attempted break-in, and the idea that it might be connected to Kathleen's belongings stuck in her mind. Could something be there that she'd missed? Maybe if she went through the things once more, she'd feel certain.

With Becca at Mavis's, she waited until Jeff's car pulled into his drive and called him. "Wonder if you'd like to do me a favor."

"Hmm? Let's see now," he teased. "What's in it for me?"

His chuckle made her smile. "Pizza and possible adventure."

"Adventure? You know I love pizza, and you're tempting me with the 'adventure' idea. Explain."

She told him the thoughts dashing through her mind.

"I think I can handle that."

"Thanks. Mavis took Becca to her house for the night. Her grandchildren are spending the night too. I thought it would be easier for Becca rather than rousing up her sadness."

"Good idea."

"We should have plenty of time to scout through the boxes again, just to make sure."

"No problem. So when's pizza?"

She gave him a time, and after hanging up, she rested against the chair, wondering how things would be without Jeff in her life.

Within a half hour he arrived, and following a meal of pizza and salad, they headed down the stairs and halted in front of the pile of boxes.

"I'm probably foolish to hang on to so much of this, but I know Becca will want the photo albums and Kathleen's high school memorabilia when she's older. I can't quite bring myself to throw some of this away."

"You don't have to, Laine. Becca can sort and decide for herself when the time comes. It doesn't hurt anything sitting here."

They each opened a box, flipping through photo albums and scrapbooks and making a pile on the floor ready for repacking when they finished.

"Look," Laine said, pulling out a small white New Testament. "This looks like one of the Bibles we got in Sunday school when we were kids." She turned the white leather binding in her hand and opened the book, gazing at the pages. "She's underlined verses and written in the margin. I had no idea Kathleen read the Bible. Studied the Bible, the way it looks." Instead of putting it on the pile, she slipped it into the oversized pocket of her blouse.

When they tackled the jewelry boxes, they sat side by side, looking for secret drawers or hidden compartments, but all their pushing and probing resulted in nothing. "I didn't think so," Laine concluded. "They look like plain old inexpensive boxes to me."

"I'd say so," Jeff agreed. "All this stuff looks exactly like 'stuff.' Nothing worth much to anyone but you and Becca." He rested his hand on the nape of her neck, kneading tenderly. "But like you said, if Scott Whatever-his-name-is thinks he left something behind, he might still be looking." He slid his hand gently down her back and turned his attention back to the box top. "If the guy was smart, he'd stay clear of you."

"I'm not sure about his 'smarts.'" She grimaced. "But he sure got away with this scam. Do you think he's still wandering around free?"

Jeff shook his head. "If we knew his real name, we could check it out."

"You and your 'check it out.'" She shook her head. "By the way, did your friend find anything on Pat?"

"Nothing yet. Pat did say her last name is 'Sorrento,' didn't she?"

"Uh-huh. Do you think it's an alias?"

"Could be. I'll talk to him again and see if he's come up with anything."

They reloaded the last boxes and piled them again in the same corner of the basement. Before they walked away, Laine paused in front of the few boxes that held her sister's life, and a wave of grief washed over her. Jeff pulled her close, and she rested her head on his shoulder, drawing strength from his presence.

"This is hard on you, Laine. In a way it's good you've been busy with Becca. It makes Kathleen's death and all your other problems take a backseat. But I'm sure tonight, plowing through the boxes, brings it all out again."

She nodded, unable to speak without sobbing.

"Ready?" He eased her away from the corner and moved her toward the stairs. "Let's go up."

"I'm okay. The truth just gives me a kick once in awhile. I feel lonely. I have Becca, and that's it. In the whole wide world, she's my only family."

"I know it's not much, but you have me too."

Standing at the foot of the stairway, he tilted her mouth to his and kissed her lightly, pressing his palm against her cheek.

She raised her arm and laid her palm against his hand,

caressing his sturdy fingers. Then she touched his face, drawing her fingers across the prickly hairs of his new beard, feeling his strong jaw tensing beneath the hair.

When they inched apart, their eyes met and held for a moment, and she drank in the depth of longing evident in his gaze. When she could take no more, she shifted toward the stairs, and they climbed with slow, easy steps, their hands tightly clasped together.

After Jeff left, Laine prepared for bed and found the Testament in her pocket. She placed it on the nightstand, and when she crawled beneath the sheet, she opened the white leather Bible and thumbed through the pages.

She halted at a dog-eared page where an underlined passage from John caught her eye: "Peace I leave with you; My peace I give you. I do not give to you as the world gives. Do not let your hearts be troubled and do not be afraid."

She imagined Kathleen's fear after Alex had died. Or maybe the fear that rose in her when she'd realized Scott wasn't all he'd led her to believe. Laine's heart weighed heavy, and she flipped a page or two before another verse from John stuck out from the page: "I have told you these things, so that in Me you may have peace. In this world you will have trouble. But take heart! I have overcome the world."

These words of Jesus had offered Kathleen comfort, and now the same words filtered through Laine's consciousness. She turned further through Acts and then to Hebrews. "So we say with confidence, 'The Lord is my helper; I will not be afraid. What can man do to me?' "

She repeated the words aloud. " 'I will not be afraid. What can man do to me?' "

Lovingly, she closed the small Testament and slid it onto the nightstand. If she read a little each night, she'd learn more about Kathleen. And perhaps something about herself.

❧

The weekend approached, leaving Laine apprehensive. Becca was to spend Saturday night with her grandmother, and Laine dreaded the event. Her thoughts swarmed like bees in and out of their hive. Would Becca be frightened or unhappy staying overnight with Glynnis? Worse, would she love it? What thoughts did Glynnis have for the future? Did she want Becca permanently? If she did, Glynnis would have to fight for her. That was certain.

But as the thoughts drummed through Laine, guilt rose as well. Glynnis could offer Becca so much—time, money, travel, education, luxuries, everything she would need to give her a good life. Then Jesus' words drifted from the back of her memory. What if a person gained the whole world and lost his soul. Were money and luxuries really that important? She thought about Scott and what he did to Kathleen, all for money. Money meant nothing if love and faith weren't the focus of a person's life.

The dreaded Saturday arrived quickly. As she waited for Glynnis's car, Laine hovered around Becca, like a mother hen over her chick. "You'll have a nice time, okay? I'm sure your grandmother has some surprises for you. And I'll see you tomorrow."

"Grandma said she'd take me out to lunch."

"That'll be fun." Laine was sure Becca had Burger Barn in mind. But Glynnis and fast food didn't jibe. A country club sounded more like Glynnis's choice for a restaurant. Laine closed her eyes, pushing away the envy and fear that jabbed at her like a bee sting.

When Glynnis arrived, Laine stood by the door and watched Becca join her grandmother without a backward glance. Penny was tucked under the little girl's arm, and Laine wondered what Glynnis thought of Becca's devotion to the raggedy thing instead of to her new doll. But Laine didn't care what Glynnis thought.

Selfish fear rose in her, and the words she'd read in Kathleen's Bible sailed through her thoughts like a banner behind a small airplane. "Do not let your hearts be troubled and do not be afraid." She needed to listen to those words.

Shortly after Becca's departure, Jeff called to rescue Laine from loneliness. "Let's enjoy the day," he said, his friendly voice filling the phone line. "How about an afternoon on the water? And then I'd like to take you to dinner. Sound okay?"

"Okay? It sounds wonderful."

"I'll meet you on the dock in a half hour."

As soon as she hung up, Laine dressed in her bathing suit, grabbed a towel and her cover-up in hand, and returned to the first floor. She had started paying more attention to security issues since the attempted break-in, and out of habit, she bolted the back door and waited for Jeff on the porch.

A burglar alarm came to mind. She'd procrastinated on getting one, though Jeff had suggested it more than once. The expense seemed foolish. Yet she'd hate to have her condo ransacked. She had little that anyone would want. But. . .

As thoughts marched through her head, Jeff appeared, heading for the dock.

Locking the repaired screen door, Laine entered the house, and after bolting the door, she exited through the garage, taking the remote opener with her. Such a fuss to protect mementos, but she didn't know what else to do.

A few minutes later, the two seated in the boat, Jeff pushed off into the glinting water. They sat in silence, soaking in the sun's warmth and listening to the soft splash of the oars dipping into the blue-green water.

Jeff's muscles tightened as he pulled the oars, sending them out into the lake and around a small island sitting near the middle. Admiration spilled into her thoughts as Laine viewed his strength, like a stanchion against all that could hurt her. Finally, she drew her attention to the small cooler he'd set into the boat, and she grinned.

"Bring your lunch?" She gestured toward the container.

"Our lunch," he corrected her. "Not lunch really but snacks. I take care of my girl."

My girl. The words rippled through her as sparkling and sunny as the tiny sun-flecked waves that danced in her eyes.

A pleasant breeze riffled through her hair, and a calm settled over her as she watched the shore drift by in the distance. In the quiet, they chatted about commonplace things, eventually heading back to the raft.

Jeff tied the boat to the mooring, helped her out, then hoisted the cooler onto the wooden platform. Spreading out a wide terry beach towel, Laine sat down, claiming one side. Without a moment to adjust to the water's temperature, Jeff dove into the lake. When his head bobbed above the water, he called to her. "Hey, it's wonderful. Trust me."

She laughed, certain the water was frigid. But she didn't argue and joined him, knifing deeply into the green lake. To her surprise, he was telling the truth. The warm, clear water wrapped around her, and her hands cut deeply through its surface.

They laughed and played like dolphins, diving down into the opalescent shimmer of light and shadow, then rising to the surface, arms clinging, lips touching. Their voices echoed on the water's surface like children in bathwater.

When they tired, Jeff climbed the ladder and reached down

to pull Laine to the raft. Sitting on the terry blanket, he stretched his legs, then lifted the cooler lid and offered her a soft drink, fresh baby carrots, cubes of cheese, and green seedless grapes as sweet and juicy as an apple.

"Not bad, kind sir. This is wonderful." She nibbled on the welcome snacks and swigged a refreshing drink of the soda.

He watched her, a pleased grin spreading across his full, sweet lips. "You look refreshed and beautiful. I worry about you. Tension is terrible, and you've had too much of it lately."

"Thanks. I feel good right now. Like I don't have a care in the world."

She flopped back on the cloth and stared into the wispy blue sky. "Not a care or a cloud. Perfect."

He lay beside her, his hand brushing her arm. "You're perfect. Well. . .almost."

She chuckled and swatted him away as if he were a fly. "I've been tense, I know. Hopefully, things will calm down. Once I know Glynnis's plans, I'll feel better. I worry she'll want to take Becca." She brushed her hair from her forehead. "I don't think I could bear it."

"Your sister wanted you to raise her. You have that on your side."

"But. . ." She rolled over on her stomach. "No one heard that but me. It's my word against Glynnis's. What if—"

"Hey, don't worry about what-ifs. They don't change a thing." His eyes sought hers, deep and penetrating, and lingered. Hesitantly, he spoke. "While we're on the subject, can I ask you a personal question?"

His words caught her by surprise, and she flinched before she could stop.

"Sorry, Laine. I'm not trying to upset you. I've wondered some things for so long and—"

"Ask me, Jeff. You've done so much for me you deserve to have your questions answered." Despite her statement, tension crept through her.

Jeff seemed to sense it, for he gently caressed her back and shoulders as he talked. "You mentioned a long time ago that you had to forgive yourself before you could be forgiven by God. I've often wondered what you meant. Whatever it is, I know it's pulled you away from your faith. . .and I'd like to understand."

Lying on her side, she propped her cheek on her hand and gazed at the lake, mesmerized by the flickering light on the water, then told him everything—her envy, her anger, her hurtful words. She sat up and crossed her legs, then told him about her sorrow and grief. "When Alex died, I felt that God had answered my prayer in the most horrible way. I'd always wanted Kathleen to know rejection and hurt. Things always seemed to sail to her on a breeze. And I. . ." She slowed, feeling the pain of grief ramrod through her body.

Jeff lifted her hand to his mouth, giving it a tender kiss. "My dearest Laine, God doesn't punish us like that." Jeff heard his words and faltered. He'd done the same, allowed his hurt and anger to heap him with sin and guilt.

She gazed at him. "But still I wasn't satisfied, you know. Even though Alex was dead, she had Becca, and there was Alex's inheritance. She didn't have to struggle to save a few dollars or get up each day to drag herself to college or to a thankless job, praying for a promotion or commendation, anything to put her up one more rung on the ladder of success."

Tears glistened in her eyes, and he rested his palms on her cheeks and wiped the tears away with his fingers. Her pain was his. He bent forward and pressed his lips on her eyelids, kissing the salty tears that clung to her lashes and wanting to let his own tears flow and cleanse his painful thoughts.

"I'm sorry," she whispered. "I don't mean to ruin our beautiful day."

"Sorry? Don't be. I asked, and you're answering. It's what I wanted. . .needed. . .to know. Thanks for telling me." Shame darted through him at questions he'd allowed to surface. Had Laine somehow been involved with Darian? He knew better, but his mind was programmed to question and search for answers. Troubleshooter. Another arrow of guilt struck his conscience.

She continued speaking as if he hadn't said a word. "The last slap was Kathleen's illness—as if God wanted to pound His punishment into my brain. I ache so badly when I think about it. My evil desires hurt my sister and Becca worse than I could ever imagine. My sin."

He forgot his earlier fears. Laine's pain weighed heavily on him. Feeling close to helpless, he sought something comforting, something hopeful that he could give her. God's love was what filled his thoughts. Forgiveness. He needed to understand and accept himself. He struggled to collect his thoughts, to organize his words, but Laine gave him what he sought.

"Remember the New Testament I found in the basement?"

He nodded.

"That night, I read some of Kathleen's underlined verses. And I've read some every night since then. The answers are there in that little white book. Forgiveness is nothing you earn. It's a gift. God's gift to us because we believe that Jesus is His Son and was sent to save sinners." She looked into his eyes, and he sensed the depth of her struggle.

"And if ever there's a sinner, it's me," she added.

"You're my angel," he said, drawing her to him. Her lips trembled, but he halted her tears with his kiss. Then he tucked her head on his shoulder and held her, his own thoughts reviewing the words she'd said. He still had so much to tell her, truths that he wasn't able to share yet. Someday he could let her know the darkness of his own anguish.

As he held her in his arms, a quivering breath eased from her, and soon she calmed, looking at him with sad but clearer eyes. "Let's not waste any more of this wonderful water," she said. "Swim?"

He nodded and helped her rise, and together they dove down into the translucent, cleansing water.

nine

Jeff drove them to a quaint, quiet spot with dim lighting and soft music. She nibbled on pâté and crackers, then enjoyed a special chicken entrée with capers and artichoke hearts on a bed of angel-hair pasta. The pasta took her back to Jeff's words—*You're my angel*—and she wrapped his loving thoughts around her.

Dinner that evening brought back Laine's smile. She tucked her sadness away, feeling cleansed and relieved. Filled and satisfied, they made their way home. Laine studied Jeff's profile in the dusky light from stores and street lamps that flickered past, grateful for his company.

"Thanks for filling my day. I kept Becca from my mind most of the time, and tomorrow she'll be back home. You've been a great friend."

"No problem. That's what I want to do always, Laine. Fill your days—our days—with good things. You know I care about you."

She nodded. "Me too." She knew she had more to say and that he did too; but they held back, each for their own reasons, she supposed. Time was one factor. They'd only known each other for a couple of months and under the worst conditions. She didn't want to misread her heart.

They rode in silence. He parked in his garage, then walked her across the grass to her condo. The moon streaked across the black water like a splash of creamy white paint. Its brightness dimmed the surrounding stars.

She hesitated as she neared the condo. A small basement window glowed in the darkness. She didn't recall being down there, not since they'd checked the boxes, and that had been a few days ago. She knew the light had been off.

"Something wrong?" Jeff halted at her side.

"The basement. There's a light on. I'm sure I didn't leave a light on down there."

"Don't start worrying already. You're getting jumpy." He slid his arm around her waist and continued toward the house. She hit the remote, and the garage door opened. Then turning the key in the inner lock, she entered.

Jeff put his hand on her back and moved around her, taking the lead. She followed him, scanning the room, but nothing seemed touched.

"It's the basement I'm wondering about." She headed toward the basement door, but again Jeff halted her. "Let me go down first, Laine. I know you're nervous."

"Thanks," she said. "For some reason, I'm really scared."

He stroked her cheek and moved around her to the top of the stairs. Halfway down, he paused, glancing back at her. "You were right. Someone was here."

"Oh, please, God, no." She darted down to join him. Kathleen's boxes were dumped and strewn in a pile, her brooches and earrings scattered on the floor, and the jewelry boxes seemed to be missing. The contents of Laine's own few cartons were also scattered around. Storage drawers were open, shelves emptied.

Laine and Jeff raced up the stairs. Her bedroom was in shambles, drawers emptied and tossed, her clothing thrown on the floor. Her own jewelry boxes were scattered on the bed. Becca's room was a jumble, toys tossed about. Her new doll lay in a heap, her dainty dress torn as if someone had stepped on it.

"I'll call the police, Laine," Jeff said as he left the room.

Entering her small office, she found desk drawers emptied in a pile. Her file cabinet was open, its contents strewn on the floor. A ragged breath tore through her. What were they after? Why the whole house?

In a minute, Jeff found her. "They're on their way." He paused, gawking at the room. "What a mess! Whoever did this came through the front window. You'll need that boarded up."

She stood frozen, surrounded by the contents of her previously neat drawers. "I don't know where to begin."

"Well, nowhere until the police come. As soon as they're here, I'll go over and check to see what I have in the garage to board up that window. I need to check my place too."

They wandered down the hall, and in a few minutes, a noise sounded in the back. Laine peeked through the kitchen door. "Looks like the police."

"Good. Then I'll run on over and see if my place is okay. I'll be back shortly." He turned and headed to the front door.

Laine's shoulders tensed as she watched the officers climb from their car. In a matter of days, she'd had to call them twice. What next? A burglar alarm, she supposed—and thought of the old saying: closing the barn door after the horse got away.

By the time Jeff returned, the police had written their reports and were gone. He brought with him a large piece of plywood and nailed it over the broken window. "We'll get this fixed tomorrow. I'm sure I can find a hardware store open somewhere."

"Thanks again. Anything wrong at your place?" Laine asked.

"Nothing. I didn't think there would be, but I didn't want to assume anything. Did the police have anything to say?"

"No. They just asked the same questions as last time. I told them about the attempt a few days ago. I suppose I need to get an alarm system."

"Maybe, but if it's not random, at least whoever did this knows now that nothing's here."

"I suppose." She shook her head, still confused and trying to understand. "I can't let Becca come back to this mess. Either I have to ask Glynnis to keep her longer or get this cleaned up as best I can tonight."

With his thumb and finger beneath her chin, Jeff tilted her face toward his. "I don't suppose you want Glynnis to keep her longer than necessary."

He always seemed to know her heart. "No, I don't."

"Then I guess we have our work cut out for us. So let's get busy."

She noticed he'd changed to a pair of jeans and a T-shirt, and she grinned. "You're way ahead of me, I see." She gestured to his clothes.

"Didn't want to waste time. I'm not going to let you do this by yourself."

"I'll be a minute. . .that is, if I can find something to put on in that mess." She turned to leave, but he touched her arm.

"What can I do here while you change?"

"Oh, thanks." She looked around. "If my files aren't too messed up, you can stack them in a pile, and I'll put them in the drawers later. When you finish there, toss the pencils and stuff back in that top drawer. Then come up, and we can tackle Becca's room."

She hurried up the stairs, changed, and gathered her strewn clothing from the floor. When she had things folded and partially in drawers again, Jeff appeared at the doorway.

"Not perfect, but I have the folders in piles. I'll start in Becca's room."

She finished taking care of her clothes and tossed her jewelry into the boxes. Hers hadn't vanished like Kathleen's. Whoever took the other boxes must have thought that maybe one had a hidden compartment.

When she joined Jeff in Becca's room, her heart sank. He'd folded most of the little girl's clothing, but her toys were a mess. With a needle and thread, Laine sat on the bed and stitched the doll's torn dress.

"Why would they tear up a child's room?" she asked, frustration flowing from her tone. "It makes me sick."

"No screaming, just keep sewing. Hopefully, she'll never notice." He rested his hand on her shoulder. "Who knows why people do crazy things?"

"God knows," she said. "God knows everything. Now, if I knew, we could get somewhere." Her hands busied themselves with the needle as her mind raced, trying to put the pieces together both literally and figuratively.

❧

Becca didn't seem to notice the torn doll dress or anything else amiss when she returned from her grandmother's. She bubbled and chattered about what they'd done and where they'd gone, and Laine felt like the custodial parent who'd sent her child off to Dad's for weekends where she was entertained and coddled and then sent back home spoiled and unhappy. She pushed her jealousy back and took time each night to read the little white New Testament.

Two weeks passed with no news from the police, but no new problems raised their ugly heads either. Other than dealing with her fears about Glynnis, Laine relaxed. Then Glynnis called and asked to meet privately.

"Leave Becca with me," Jeff suggested. "It's only an hour or two. We always have a good time together. And stop worrying.

It's not necessarily gloom and doom."

"I know, but I can't help it. I relax, and bang! Something else goes wrong. I'll go and get it over with, I guess. I'll call her back and arrange it for the weekend."

Glynnis agreed, and Saturday Laine walked Becca, clutching Penny to her chest, to Jeff's, then drove to Glynnis's with her heart beating in her throat. Fear gripped her, wondering what Glynnis had in mind. Though they'd cooperated with each other so far, Glynnis had money to fight Laine in court, and Laine still struggled with the difficult question: What was best for her niece?

The imperious house rose in front of her, and with trepidation she climbed the three brick steps to the fanlight door. The housekeeper greeted her and guided her in. An air of formality hung in the foyer, and Laine's breath tripped inside her as she headed for the familiar living room.

Glynnis sat in her usual chair, like a queen on her throne. A tray of scones and carafe of tea or coffee lay waiting for her arrival. "Good morning, Laine," Glynnis said as her guest entered the room.

Becca's grandmother rose and gestured to the chair where Laine had sat on her other visits. Laine eyed it questioningly, looking for the straps to tie her down and gas pellets to end her life. An ominous feeling clung to her—whether reality or fantasy, only time would tell.

"How are you, Glynnis?" Her voice caught, and a telltale tremor gave it an alien sound. She sat on the edge of her chair across from the elderly woman.

Glynnis looked older than usual. Though a tasteful hint of blush colored her cheeks and her hair neatly framed her face, something seemed different. Perhaps the look in her eyes.

"So," Laine said, directing her gaze. She crossed her leg,

but it trembled so obviously, she lowered it again. "You had something to discuss?"

"Yes, but first have some coffee and a scone. They're fresh and very delicious."

The last meal. Laine couldn't swallow a scone if her life depended on it, but she accepted the coffee, controlling her quaking fingers until the cup rested at her side. The woman's gaze penetrated hers, and Laine sat rigid and waiting.

"I've been giving Rebecca's situation a great deal of thought. I realize we've avoided the topic, but school begins in a few weeks, and we should have things settled by then."

"Yes, we should." The words exited her in a whisper.

"Rebecca is all that I have left of my son. Yet I realize that your sister placed her in your care. I want us to do what is best for the child."

"We must, yes," Laine agreed, but the edging fear nailed her to the chair. She heard the beginning of a discussion she hoped she would never hear.

"I have the means to provide Rebecca with many good things. Though I'm elderly, I can hire a young nanny, and I can provide the best schools. Rebecca seems comfortable here. I enjoy her company. She's a lovely, well-behaved child." Her eyes softened. "Kathleen, I must say, was an excellent parent."

"Thank you. I know she was." Laine swallowed hard, forcing back the emotion rising within her. "But please remember that Becca is all I have left of my family—sister, parents. Becca is all I have."

"I know." She paused, lowering her eyes to her dainty china cup. "But we must think of what's best for her." She looked at her again, filled with new energy. "I realize you're young. You have vitality and stamina that I don't have. But you work every day. I'm here. You'll marry and have children of your own. That day is long past for me."

Laine closed her eyes, pushing back tears of reality that struggled for release.

"I believe that Rebecca would benefit from living here," Glynnis continued. "You would certainly have her for weekends, time in the summer, whenever. I'll be happy to share our time. I know you love her and want what is best for her. What I am asking is that you think about what I'm saying. We need to decide soon—before school begins. Whatever we do, I hope it will be in cooperation, rather than in opposition. I'm asking you to think about this."

Laine couldn't speak, and though she struggled, tears hedged from her eyes and tickled down her cheeks. "I have been doing just that, Glynnis. Over and over. But I can't bear the thought of losing her."

"You are not losing Rebecca. You'd be sharing her with someone who loves her as dearly as you do." A faint grin lifted the corner of Glynnis's mouth. "We had lunch at a fast-food restaurant last week."

Laine's heart dipped and rose, and a laugh burst from her, bordering on hysteria. She snatched it back quickly, controlling it to a chuckle. "It's hard to imagine, but I understand what you're saying."

"Will you give some thought to what I've said?"

Laine's shoulder lifted in a desperate sigh. "Yes, I will, and I have. Oh, dearest Lord, I have." Her words were her prayer.

ten

Laine tossed all hope of control aside when she reached her car. The love and fear she'd struggled to keep buried burst like a dam, pouring anguish and desperation through her. With blurry eyes, she drove back to the condo. Thoughts and questions piled in a precarious mound in front of her, waiting to topple and bury her beneath their confusion.

How could she look at Becca without grabbing her in her arms and holding her in a death grip? The impending feeling of loss and loneliness washed over her. She had to do what was best for the child. She needed to think clearly. She needed to pray.

Pulling into the garage, she saw Jeff across the lawn visiting with someone. She needed time to sort through her problems and longed to speak with Jeff alone. She closed the garage door, entering her condo through the kitchen. She needed to get a grip on herself before she went to him.

She changed her clothes and ran a cold cloth over her face and eyes, then adjusted her smeared makeup. She looked stressed but presentable. If she could only stay that way.

As she crossed the lawn, her heart sank. Pat sat in a chair beneath the tree. Becca leaned on the arm, apparently chattering as she often did. Why was Pat here again? And always when she wasn't home? Pushing a pleasant expression to her lips, she continued forward but knew her eyes told the truth.

Becca darted across the grass to meet her. Laine drew the child into her arms, struggling to keep her grip natural. When she reached the chairs, she added a congenial lilt to her voice. "Pat, how are you?"

"Fine, but how are you?"

Her face looked concerned, and Laine wondered if Jeff had told her about the meeting with Glynnis. The thought irritated her. "I'm okay. Why do you ask?"

"Jeff told me about the. . .to-do the other evening." She glimpsed at Becca.

Laine relaxed slightly. "Yes, I've recovered just fine."

Becca swung her head from one woman to the other, appearing to know they were talking over her head. Laine ruffled her hair and sat in a chair beside them, her arms around Becca, who leaned against her.

Pat glimpsed at her watch. "Well, I hadn't heard from anyone and was passing this way, so I decided to stop and see how everyone was." She tilted her head and smiled at Becca. "I can't believe you're starting school in a few weeks. You've grown up too fast."

At the word "school," Laine's heart twisted. Memory of her conversation with Glynnis jolted through her. "She is, isn't she?" Laine said. "Becca and I have to do some shopping for school clothes in a few days."

"Yippee!" Becca said, clapping her hands. "I get new clothes, and you said a schoolbag."

"Sure thing," Laine agreed. "What's school without a schoolbag?" She sensed she was being overly exuberant. Jeff gave her a questioning look.

Pat rose and stood in front of the canvas chair. "Well, I'd better be on my way. Nice talking to you, Jeff. And good to see you too, Laine." She smiled down at Becca. "Hey, Kiddo, give me a kiss, huh?"

She leaned down, and the child planted a kiss on Pat's cheek.

With a wave, the woman headed for her car, parked in front of Jeff's condo. Becca skipped along with her to the sidewalk.

Jeff saw the pain and hurt in Laine's eyes but waited for Pat to leave before asking what happened. "Didn't go well, huh?"

"No. She wants Becca."

He saw her swallow back the tears, but the battle was lost, despite her efforts, and she wiped them away with her fingers.

"She wants us to cooperate and asked me to think about it." She lifted her brows, her eyes widened. "As if I haven't thought about it a hundred times."

"At least she's taking your feelings into consideration."

"Her arguments are good ones, Jeff. But I don't know that I can do what she's asking. I'm trying to think of Becca, but my own selfish needs stab at me. I can't bear it."

Her grief stirred his own sadness. He rose and knelt by her side. "Listen, I wish I could be with you tonight. I just got a call awhile ago, and I have to get back to work. Let's take time tomorrow to think this through clearly and logically. Okay?"

Silently she nodded, and he understood. If she spoke, her sobs would take over. Seeing Becca heading their way, Jeff touched Laine's hand. "She's coming back, so get yourself under control." He shifted back into the chair and grinned at Becca.

Becca bounded back, waving currency in her hand. "Look what Aunt Pat gave me. Ten dollars! For school clothes."

Jeff opened his arms, giving Becca a hug and giving Laine time to get a grip on herself. "Wow! You are a lucky girl to have so many people love you."

"I'm lovable. That's what my grandma says."

Laine's grin looked feeble. "Everyone thinks you're lovable, Sweetheart."

Becca spun around and gave Laine a bear hug, kissing her

cheek. "Would you hold my money so I won't lose it?"

Jeff only half-listened to the two chatter. His mind was distracted by the information he'd learned from Pat. So many questions were answered. So many new questions were formulated. What would he do now? Things were moving in, and what he'd kept hidden weighed him down. He wanted so badly to speak the truth to Laine, but he wasn't free to do that. Not until it was all over.

❧

That evening, Laine curled on her bed, tears running from her eyes. If only Jeff were there to listen. Yet she held the white Testament in her hand, seeking its comfort. Kathleen's underlined words had become hers. Over and over, she read Jesus' words found in John: "Peace I leave with you; My peace I give you. I do not give to you as the world gives. Do not let your hearts be troubled and do not be afraid."

She flipped through the pages, going back to a verse in Matthew. When she saw Kathleen's underline, she halted, running her finger along the sentence—a sentence that meant more than anything at this moment: "If you believe, you will receive whatever you ask for in prayer."

Laine closed her eyes and prayed fervently. She needed strength and courage to do what the Lord wanted her to do and freedom from the fear of the stranger who wanted something she didn't understand. She feared for Becca and for herself. When she whispered her "amen," a quiet peace drifted over her. She laid the Testament on the table and snapped off the light, letting sleep engulf her.

When the morning light peeked through the window, Laine woke with a gasp and sat on the edge of the bed. She'd slept the night through without waking. Though she needed the sleep, she worried if she would have heard anything if something had happened, if someone had broken in again. She would have, she was sure.

She reached toward the Testament and opened the pages, her eyes scanning the words Kathleen had marked, but she read further. Verse after verse, God's Word was renewing her lost faith. She finally grasped the meaning of forgiveness, and she better understood human weakness. As her flaws became clearer, she faced the need to forgive herself. But she knew in her heart, God had forgiven her already.

Her fingers slid along the inside of the back cover, and for some reason, she opened the Testament to the back page. She'd never noticed before. Kathleen had written down an Old Testament verse from Isaiah: "I will give you the treasures of darkness, riches stored in secret places, so that you may know that I am the LORD."

Why? What did this verse mean to Kathleen? Riches stored in secret places. The words tugged at Laine and made her wish she could search through the jewelry boxes for secret compartments again. . .but they were taken during the break-in. Below the verse, Kathleen had written two Bible references—one from 2 Corinthians and one from 1 Peter. She riffled through the thin pages, looking for the first reference.

"Aunt Laine," Becca called from the hall. "I'm hungry."

She stopped and glanced at the clock on her nightstand. If she didn't move immediately, they'd miss Sunday school. She laid the Testament back on the stand. Later, she'd find the verses. Now she'd better get some food in Becca and get them both ready for church.

❧

Arriving at the church, Laine pushed Becca toward Sunday school, but the child's fingers clutched hers, half-dragging her toward the classroom. She caught on in a heartbeat.

Becca wanted her to help again in Sunday school.

As they came through the door, Sue smiled at them, focusing first on Becca, then lifting her questioning gaze to Laine. "Did you want to help me again today?" she asked.

Laine opened her mouth to say no, but before she could utter a sound, Becca shot out her answer. "She'll help. Okay, Auntie Laine?" The child looked at her with pleading eyes.

Wondering if she was making a big mistake by letting Becca manipulate the situation, Laine had no real time to reach any conclusion. She was caught in the middle. "If you need help, I'll stay," Laine said, pushing a pleasant grin to her face. "But only if you really need the help."

"I can always use help." Sue hesitated, then her expression crumbled. "Actually, you're saving the day. My helper has decided coming to Sunday school and church takes too much effort, so I'm really shorthanded. I could use a permanent assistant."

"Permanent?" Laine felt the guillotine pressing against her neck.

Sue's shoulders lifted shyly, and the look of chagrin reflected on her mottled cheeks.

Laine glowered down at Becca. But the child's face glowed with happiness, and suddenly Laine's scowl melted to a grin. How could she say no to either of the pleading faces that gazed at her?

"I can only give it a try," she said.

Sue's dismal expression broke into a smile. "Thanks. What a relief!"

Laine shuddered a sigh, lifting her eyes heavenward. She assumed the Lord, as well as Becca, was at work. With the situation out of her hands, Laine delved into her first day as an official Sunday-school assistant.

ක

Arriving home from church, Becca claimed she was starving. Laine acknowledged that breakfast had been skimpy, to say the least. So as Becca headed in to change from her Sunday clothes, Laine remained in the kitchen, still dressed in her silky shirtdress and pumps. As she cracked the first egg into the bowl, Jeff's voice called from outside the porch. "Unlock, I'm here."

She hurried to the screen door, unhooking the latch, and Jeff stepped in, blurry eyed but smiling. "Sorry I couldn't be here for you yesterday."

Laine shrugged. "Work is work. I just wondered why you had to go in on a Saturday night."

He draped his hand on her shoulder. "It was a hot job. You know how that is. How are things going today?"

"Okay. Trying not to think about it." She forced a half-hearted grin. "We just got home from church."

He paused and gazed at her for a moment as if seeing her for the first time that morning. "You look better than okay. You sure look great."

"Thanks," she said, "but you aren't going to sweet-talk me. What do you really want?"

He didn't answer, instead slipping his arm around her waist as she guided him back to the kitchen. Stepping through the door, Jeff gave her a squeeze. "I arrived at a perfect time, huh? Breakfast."

"I should have guessed what you wanted. You can smell something not even on the stove yet?"

"I know. It's a man's thing, I guess. We have a seventh sense."

"Scents—s-c-e-n-t-s—is right! But seventh? What happened to the sixth?"

"Women seem to have that." Playfully, he bumped her with his hip. "Let me do these eggs. You go change your clothes, and then do whatever else needs doing."

She bumped him back and hurried from the room. If she didn't change, she'd have grease stains on her clean dress, for sure.

When she returned, Jeff was beating eggs, and she opened the refrigerator for the sausage links. Working side by side, a sense of completeness washed over her. Becca changing clothes in her room, Jeff helping her in the kitchen, it felt right and good, the way God meant life to feel.

"Jeff!" Becca squealed, darting into the room.

Her noisy entrance sent Laine's thoughts out the window.

"Aunt Laine is my pernament Sunday-school helper."

Jeff lifted at eyebrow and gazed at Laine. "You? The pernament helper, huh?"

"That word is 'permanent,' Becca." She turned the sausages in the pan.

Becca repeated her. "Permanent."

"Right." She glowered at Jeff, letting him know he'd better not make a single comment, and with a dramatic thud, she popped bread in the toaster and pulled out two mugs.

Jeff ducked playfully and didn't say a single word.

Already the scent of fresh coffee filled the room, and Laine's appetite finally returned with a vengeance.

The meal vanished in less time than it took to think about making it, and Becca wandered off to play. As soon as she left the room, Jeff's hand grasped Laine's. He pulled it to his lips with a kiss, then held it tenderly. "So let's talk while we have a moment. You look so happy, I hate to bring it up. But things need to be said."

He was right. Pushing the problem away while he was

there was foolish. Happiness surrounded her now, but later in the day when she was alone, the thoughts would haunt her again. She told him, as calmly as she could, the details of her conversation with Glynnis, her logical thoughts, her sorrows and fears.

His gaze caressed her face as tenderly as his fingers brushed the skin of her hand. She sensed his own emotions as he listened. Nuances of feeling moved across his strong, manly face, and though tears didn't pour from his eyes, she sensed them puddling in his heart.

"I hear everything you're saying, Laine. But I wonder about the priorities. Money doesn't give a child everything she needs. A nanny is one thing, but a mother substitute—a loving aunt—is another. Glynnis is her grandmother, yes. But how long will she be around to stand by Becca's side?"

"I've thought of that. But none of us know how much time we have, Jeff. Look at Kathleen."

He grimaced. "I guess you're right. We don't know for sure. I have no doubt Glynnis loves her deeply. Wherever Becca is, she won't be without love."

"I have a hard time separating Becca's needs from mine—knowing what's best for her rather than what's best for me. I've been reading Kathleen's New Testament over and over. I'm wearing out the pages."

"That can't hurt." He squeezed her fingers gently. "Maybe God used this awful situation to reel you back in, Laine."

"I've thought of that too." The little Testament stayed in her thoughts, and she remembered Kathleen's penciled references on its back page. "Wait a minute. I want to show you something."

She rose and returned quickly with the New Testament. "Look at this verse Kathleen wrote from the Old Testament.

What do you think?"

He read her scrawled words and frowned. "I'm not sure. Maybe she realized Derian was after her money and jewelry."

"That could be it. What I saw was the reference to 'hidden in secret places.' I thought about us searching for hidden compartments in her jewelry boxes weeks ago."

He tapped his fingers against the tabletop. "Right, and so did whoever broke in here. He must've had a similar idea."

"Anyway, there's more. See, she's written references here." Taking the book from Jeff, Laine turned to the first verse Kathleen had noted. They scanned the words together. Phrases jumped out at Laine: "do not lose heart. . .wasting away. . .being renewed day by day. . .momentary troubles. . . eternal glory that far outweighs them all."

She pointed to the words. "Kathleen knew she was dying. There's no question." She ached for her sister's lonely suffering.

Pressure pushed against her throat, but as she continued reading the verse, the last words caught her attention: "So we fix our eyes not on what is seen, but on what is unseen. For what is seen is temporary, but what is unseen is eternal."

Things unseen? Earlier she'd read "stored in secret places." "Look at these words, Jeff. Was Kathleen saying something? Or is my imagination too vivid?"

"I don't know, Laine, but I see what you're saying. It makes you wonder. But don't get your hopes up. 'Things unseen' refers to God's grace and mercy—salvation."

"I know, but it's the particular words that makes me wonder. " 'Things unseen.' I just can't help thinking it means something." Her pulse raced as she hunted through 1 Peter, the next reference. "Listen to this: 'Your beauty should not come from outward adornment, such as braided hair and the wearing of gold jewelry and fine clothes. Instead, it should be that of your inner self, the unfading beauty of a gentle and quiet spirit, which is of great worth in God's sight.' "

She heard him take a deep breath. "Are you thinking what I am? The jewelry? The diamonds? Is there a connection?"

Jeff rubbed his hand along her arm. "Maybe she's saying she got rid of the jewelry. Or she might mean nothing at all. If she knew she was dying, perhaps she was reminding herself that her faith and beliefs were more important than a jewel in God's sight. That could be all she's saying."

Laine stared at the words. While Jeff had a point, in her heart, she believed Kathleen was sending her or someone a message.

eleven

When Laine arrived home from work on Monday, she did everything except call Glynnis. Jeff's words sat in her mind, and like the scale of justice, she piled one set of possibilities on one side and another set on the other. The balance was precarious. It could be tipped either way by a breath of wind.

School was fast approaching, and shopping was a needed and useful escape. After dinner, with Becca in tow, Laine entered the nearest mall. They headed for the popular department store where a "school sale" banner draped across the entrance. Wandering down the aisles, Laine felt distracted, but Becca skipped along, excited to be shopping for her first school clothes.

Laine knew school shopping was a dreaded task for many a parent, but Becca was so young. Shopping with a five year old, she thought, couldn't be that difficult. But it wasn't long before she was gaping in amazement as Becca turned her nose up at one outfit after another. She didn't like the color. This dress was for little girls. Stripes going sideways looked silly. She didn't like tops that were tight around her neck— one problem after another. Though Laine tried to be firm, Becca's distinct fashion style made her grin. Her niece knew what she wanted.

After trying on numerous mix-and-match pieces, they'd only agreed on two sets. Laine gave up on outer garments and found undergarments an easier sell. A new pair of shoes was added to their purchases, and finally, they found their way to the book bags.

Here, Laine gave Becca free rein, and she enjoyed every minute, trying them on, checking the pockets, selecting the color, and unzipping, unsnapping, and unhooking everything. Laine snickered at her antics until, with bright smiles, they headed to the checkout counter.

"Could we have a treat?" Becca asked as Laine signed the charge-card bill.

"Treat? What do you call all this stuff in these bags?"

Becca giggled. "School clothes and stuff."

"Ah, and you want a food treat."

She nodded her head, a sly grin on her lips.

"I thought we just had dinner a short time ago. How about a soft drink?"

"Is that all?" A playful pout pulled on her bottom lip.

Laine gave her a wink. "We could have an ice cream."

Becca's head bobbed up and down like a paddleball.

Balancing her bulky packages, Laine clutched Becca's hand and guided her through the mall. As they headed for the small snack bar, her heart lurched.

She faltered.

Turning quickly away, she blocked the view and rounded a corner. Becca noticed everything, and her questioning gaze swept over Laine's face. "What's wrong? The snack place is that way." She pointed back through the mall.

"I know, but I have to sit for a minute and get organized." Laine slumped to a nearby bench, her hands trembling. Becca's perceptive eyes watched her, but she asked no more questions.

Laine opened her sacks, putting smaller parcels in larger bags, anything to pass time while she thought. She had seen Jeff seated inside the coffee shop around the corner. Pat sat across from him. They leaned together talking, looking deeply into each other's eyes. What did it mean? No matter what the answer might be, she decided it wasn't what she wanted to hear. She couldn't believe they were dating secretly. But she remembered Pat had focused an admiring eye on Jeff the first day they'd met. She'd stared at him with interest. But who wouldn't? Laine had passed it off.

Suddenly, Laine viewed Pat's visit with Jeff and Becca a few days earlier differently. If Pat had come to see Becca, why had she parked at Jeff's? When Becca had run to kiss the woman good-bye, Laine recalled distinctly that Pat's car had been in front of Jeff's condo, not hers. Laine's heart hammered.

So what did it mean? Were they working together? Partners in some kind of con game? Lately she'd become suspicious of everything. She couldn't believe they were the people who'd broken into her condo looking for Kathleen's jewelry or money that Laine wasn't even sure existed. She'd felt uneasy around Pat from the first day when she'd showed up unannounced at her house. She'd never understood why, but that's how she felt.

Yet she hadn't suspected Jeff. He was different. He'd been helpful. He'd even told her his friend would check on Pat. Was that only a cover-up? Laine closed her eyes, feeling betrayed and forsaken. She didn't know where to turn.

Jeff had spoken of God and forgiveness. Was it all a lie? Was his affection for her a lie? Was she another Kathleen, blindly trusting a man because she needed a friend? Needed someone to love? Her mind swirled like a raging river, and she was caught in the swift, surging current.

"Auntie, let's go," Becca urged.

Impelled by Becca's pleading, she rose on trembling knees and retraced her steps toward the small snack stand near the parking entrance. What would she say to Jeff? If he were lying, whom could she turn to?

Whom could she turn to?

All the way home through Becca's chatter, Laine sorted out her thoughts. She didn't want to see Jeff. How could she avoid him? A plan began to formulate. She needed time to think. When she arrived home, she'd call Mavis and see if Becca could spend the night. Mavis could bring her home in the morning.

Then what? She didn't have a friend in the world except Jeff, and now. . .now she didn't have a friend in the world. She had to stay away from the house, away from him. At least until she could make sense out of what she'd just seen.

She forced herself to move calmly so as not to frighten Becca. She made the call first. When she hung up from talking with Mavis, she called Becca. "Guess what?"

Becca shrugged.

"You're going to spend the night with Mrs. Dexter."

Her face wrinkled with a scowl. "Why?"

"Because I have some things to do, and I know you don't want me to drag you all over town. You'll have lots more fun at Mrs. Dexter's. Okay?"

"I guess." She shrugged again, looking disappointed.

"Let's throw some PJs in your new backpack."

The backpack idea cheered Becca up. After tossing clean clothes and pajamas into the canvas bag, Laine had the little girl gather up a couple special toys, and she slipped into her own room.

Glancing through her closet, she looked for something to put her clothes in. The last thing she wanted to do was scare Becca by leaving with a piece of luggage. She found an old duffel bag, and pulling it from the closet, she packed what she needed for work the following day. She'd stay away tonight.

She was being overly dramatic maybe, but she couldn't handle anything more tonight.

At the last minute, she placed the New Testament into the bag, zipping it closed. Laine looked around her bedroom one last time to make sure she hadn't forgotten anything. She rubbed her neck, planted a pleasant look on her face, then hurried toward the kitchen. As she came through the doorway, Becca skipped toward her with a white envelope in her hand.

"What's that, Sweetheart?"

Curious, Becca turned the paper over in her fingers. "I found it pushed under the porch door."

Laine held out her hand, her hopes lifting. "It's probably from Jeff." Becca handed her the note, and she slipped open the sealed envelope. She prayed there was an explanation from him, something to explain his meeting Pat, something that would make her present plan seem foolish and stupid. Instead, a gasp shot from her without thinking.

Becca's face paled, and she grabbed Laine's skirt. "What's wrong?" She clung to Laine's arm.

"I'm sorry, Sweetie. The note surprised me, that's all. Nothing's wrong." She glanced at the child's face, realizing that her false words had only lightened Becca's fear. The girl's grip on Laine's forearm remained uncomfortably tight.

Laine shoved the note into her pocket, hoping she appeared casual. "It's from Jeff. He has to work again tonight. I just feel sorry for him."

"Me too," Becca agreed, accepting her explanation.

"Well, we'd better get going. Mrs. Dexter's expecting us."

Laine moved calmly, though her heart raced as if she were in a high-speed chase. The note might have been from Jeff, but it certainly didn't match what she had told Becca. It was an ominous threat. No demands. No ransom. Nothing. Only the words: "You or the kid knows where the diamonds are. You can't hide them much longer."

Was she right? Were Jeff and Pat in this together? Even as she considered the idea, her heart screamed no. The whole thing made no sense. She knew nothing. Becca knew nothing. What was she to do?

After she planted Becca safely at Mavis's, Laine headed for the police station. Without Jeff's guidance, she couldn't ignore the message. And now, she couldn't trust Jeff. Stating her business, she was directed to an officer she recognized as one of the men who'd come following the break-in.

He read the note and looked at her. "No idea where this came from then?" he asked.

"My niece found it tonight on the porch, slipped under the screen door. Naturally, my first thought was that it came from the man I told you about the night of the break-in."

He scanned the report he'd pulled from the file drawer. "Scott Derian, huh?"

"Yes. He conned my sister out of a great deal of money. I explained that before."

He nodded. "I see it here in the report." He eyed her. "Why didn't your sister notify the police about this?"

Laine shrugged. "I don't know. Afraid of retribution? Humiliated? Ashamed of her gullibility? Your guess is as good as mine."

"You should have insisted."

"Yes, I suppose. But I lived far away then." Excuses. How could she tell him she'd harbored bad feelings toward her sister then? That she'd avoided contact with her?

"So what's your second thought?"

She frowned, squinting at him. "What do you mean?"

"You said your first thought was Scott Derian. What was your second thought?"

Had she really said 'first thought'? Jeff or Pat or both was her second thought. "I'm not sure what I meant. . .exactly."

His eyes narrowed. "Could you give it a try?" He folded his arms and leaned back in his chair, staring at her.

Was he interrogating her? All he needed was the spotlight. "What do you want me to say? I didn't write the note myself."

"Answer my question. What's your second thought? We can't help you if you don't give us all the information."

A pain shot up her neck from her tensed shoulders. She flinched and closed her eyes. When she opened them, his penetrating gaze remained locked on hers. "My neighbor, I suppose. And my sister's friend. . .a Pat Sorrento."

Her heart aching, she told him about Jeff and Pat, her suspicions, her fears. With each word, her heart grew heavier, the sense of loss overwhelming. She'd grown to depend on Jeff. He'd become her best friend, really her only friend since she'd returned to Michigan. Though she had coworkers, they remained just that. She hadn't shared a moment with them outside the office. With Kathleen's death, Becca's arrival, and all the complications, Jeff had stepped into her world and been her mainstay. Without him, she felt lost.

The officer scribbled the information on a form, asking an occasional question and appearing bored. When she finished, drained and depressed, he tossed the clipboard on his desk. "I guess that's it for now. If we have any other questions, we'll contact you at one of the numbers you gave us."

When she stepped out into the muggy August evening, her heart felt as dark as the night sky. A sense of sadness pervaded every step, every thought. Not knowing what to do, she headed for the highway closest to her office, searching for a motel. She'd spend the night there. If she went home, Jeff might try to talk to her. She couldn't handle that tonight.

Once in her rented room, she struggled to make sense out of everything that had happened. Pieces of the puzzle began to fit together. Why hadn't she noticed that Jeff always vanished when the police arrived at her condo? One day she'd questioned him about doing something illegal, and he'd beguiled her just like Scott had beguiled her sister. "I wouldn't do anything illegal," he'd said, and she'd believed him.

Fool. Silly, gullible fool. The problem was genetic. How could she criticize Kathleen for falling in love with a con man when she'd done the same thing?

Awareness shivered through her like ice. Could it be? Was Jeff in with Scott Darian? Was he part of the gang who preyed on innocent women? She remembered the sadness in Jeff's eyes when he spoke of his mother. Was that a fabrication? Did he think she'd trust him, believe him, after she'd heard his tale?

She sank into the cushion like a pin-pricked balloon. She had believed him. She'd even hesitated to ask him for details about his mother, fearing she would only cause him more pain. Laine knew she'd been a fool.

A lonely fool. Sorrow pressed against her heart, and she felt empty.

An indescribable loneliness filled her. Then she recalled the New Testament, and pulling it from the bottom of the duffel bag where it had settled, she lay across the bed, searching the pages for words to give her courage and strength.

Then it came to her—the answer. Here was her friend. In all of her new faith awareness, at the moment of crisis, she'd forgotten what she'd learned. Jesus was her friend. A friend she could count on. Her prayer began, and before the "amen" was uttered, she felt sleep weighing on her eyes.

In the light of morning, Laine woke with new thoughts.

She didn't have the answers, but she had to move forward. She dressed, then grabbing coffee and a bagel at a small café, she headed for work.

But that morning work didn't hold her thoughts. She spent more time doodling and struggling to keep her fears pushed away. When the telephone rang, she jumped and grabbed the receiver, identifying herself.

"This is Sergeant Dickson. Are your sure the woman's last name is 'Sorrento?'"

"As far as I know. Why?" She frowned into the telephone.

"I'm just verifying. We'll keep checking."

She put down the receiver, sensing what she'd suspected all along. "Sorrento" wasn't Pat's real name.

The phone's shrill peal caught her off guard again. She waited for the third ring, then lifted the receiver.

"Laine, this is Jeff. Where have you been?"

Ice ran through her. "I had business to take care of."

"But it's not like you. I've been worried."

"Sorry. I was in a hurry." Her voice sounded monotone and lifeless.

"Something's wrong. I can tell by your voice. Can't you talk? Is someone there?"

Her stomach tightened. His game nauseated her. "I can talk, Jeff. I have nothing to say."

"Please, Laine. I know something's wrong. Meet me for lunch. Tell me what's frightening you. What's going on?"

His voice pleaded, but she wouldn't fall for it. She'd let him con her before but not this time. "Jeff, I'm at work and busy. I really can't talk now."

A lengthy pause stretched across the phone line. She heard his sigh. "I can't make you tell me, Laine. I'll see you tonight. Please, don't do anything you'll regret."

The telephone clicked, and she sat immobile. Don't do anything you'll regret. Was this another threat? Her hand trembled as she replaced the receiver. What was he planning? What did he want of her?

twelve

All the way home, Laine thought of Becca. More and more, reality stared her down. Becca wasn't safe with her. Glynnis had the safest haven, the greatest advantages, the most logical home for the little girl. The pressure weighed on Laine's shoulders, and her head pounded with the truth. All she could offer Becca was love. Her grandmother could give her that and much more.

Though sorrow spilled from her with the force of Niagara Falls, her decision was made. She prayed Becca would understand that the reason she was giving the little girl to her grandmother was because of the things her grandmother could provide that Laine simply couldn't. Glynnis had said Laine and Becca could have weekends together, time together. The thought didn't soothe Laine. Tears rolled from her eyes, dripping to her hands, which clutched the steering wheel. Laine had lived before without Becca in her daily life. She'd learn to live again.

Somehow.

Entering the house, silence struck her. She smelled food cooking, so she knew Mavis had to be somewhere close by. Hurrying into the living room, she saw Mavis sitting in a chair.

The woman looked up in surprise. "Oh, sorry, I didn't hear you come in." She folded her magazine. "I have a chicken casserole in the oven."

Laine felt as if she were in a trance. "Where's Becca?" Her

gaze darted around the room, her ears searching for the child's voice.

"She's outside playing. Is something wrong?"

"No. I'm sorry. I'm not feeling well." She glanced toward the screened porch. "Thanks, Mavis. I'll feel better later."

"If you're sure." The woman eyed her.

"I'm sure," she said, not wanting to talk about her fears.

"Don't forget the casserole." Mavis glanced at her wristwatch. "The timer should go off in about twenty-five minutes or so." She studied her again, finally turning toward the kitchen.

"Okay, thanks," Laine called after her.

She heard the back door close and hurried out to the porch. Scanning the front, she couldn't see Becca anywhere. Then she heard her laughter coming from the next yard. She stepped from the screened porch and saw Becca with Jeff. The child giggled, tugging on his arm. Then she let go and ran from him as he chased her in circles, her screeches and giggles soaring across the grass.

Laine flew through the yard toward them. Jeff looked up and stopped, frozen. She heard herself screeching Becca's name. The child halted in midlaughter. Jeff and Becca peered at Laine, their mouths gaping as if she'd become some wildcat bounding toward its prey.

"Becca, I said come here," Laine yelled.

Though Becca faltered, she turned and ran toward Laine. "What's wrong?" she questioned, fright sounding in her voice.

"Nothing's wrong. I need you at home." She jerked her by the arm and tugged her across the grass.

Jeff yelled out and raced toward them. "Laine, stop. What in the world is wrong with you?" He reached out and caught her by the arm. "Please, stop."

She tugged without success, trying to break free from his powerful grip. "Let go of me."

"No, tell me what's wrong with you."

Becca's sobs brought Laine to her senses. She looked down at the child, wiping her eyes with her hands, tears rolling down her face. She knelt down and wrapped her arms around the frightened girl, ashamed of the scene she had caused and the fear she had created. "It's all right, Becca. I'm sorry. I didn't mean to frighten you."

Jeff knelt beside her. His pleading voice whispered in her ears as she comforted Becca. And her mind heard a swirling mixture of her voice and his.

"What is it, Laine?" he whispered. "What's wrong?"

Laine swung to face him. "Not now. I'll talk to you later. Becca is more important."

She stood, holding the child against her skirt, and they hurried across the lawn and into the house with Jeff staring after them, unmoving.

Inside, shame filled her as she held Becca in her arms, trying to conjure up a reasonable explanation to soothe her. She'd had a bad day at work. Something happened on the way home that had scared her. She was sorry, and she loved her. Laine rocked Becca, clasping the child against her heaving chest. Her own fear and confusion mounted with each moment.

At last Becca calmed down, and when the buzzer sounded, Laine guided her to the kitchen. Hunger had deserted her, and she pushed the chicken casserole around on her plate. Becca nibbled but ate little. How could she blame the child? She'd created a mess with her hysteria. She had to get a grip on herself and think logically.

Distracting Becca with games and stories, the two hours before the girl's bedtime passed quickly. But tucking Becca in brought a new dilemma. Penny was nowhere to be found. Finally, Becca recalled taking her to Jeff's.

"Sweetheart, she'll be safe with Jeff, and we can get her tomorrow. Okay? It's too late now. Let me give you Grandma Keary's doll."

Shaking her head, Becca whimpered, "But I want Penny."

Laine had to stand her ground. "It's this dolly or none. Penny won't be home until tomorrow."

The child rolled over without the new doll, and Laine tucked her in, kissing her on the cheek. Laine snapped off the light and tiptoed out.

She sat in the living room, wishing she'd listened to Jeff, but how could she believe him now? Indistinctly, she heard a noise coming from the porch. The hairs bristled on her arms, and she froze, her hands clinging to the arms of the chair.

"Laine. It's me. Please let me in."

Jeff's whisper drifted through the screens. She relaxed, hearing his voice, but tension surged again, remembering. Not wanting him to disturb Becca, she pushed herself up from the chair on trembling legs and walked to the doorway.

"Not tonight, Jeff, please. I'm very upset, and I'll say things I might regret."

"If I did something, you owe me an opportunity to explain or apologize, please. I'd never do anything to hurt you. I know you're angry, but please tell me what it is. How can I help you if I don't know what's wrong?"

His pleading only confused her further. She didn't know which course to take or where things were headed. But one thing she knew, if she were to trust God's Word, she owed Jeff an opportunity to speak and at least ask her forgiveness for his lies. "You can come on the porch, Jeff, but only for a few minutes."

She unhooked the latch, and he entered, keeping his distance. In his eyes, she saw the desire to take her in his arms, and she had to admit her natural desire was to go to him.

"You can sit if you want." She gestured to a chair.

He slumped down, staring up at her, and she sank nearby and focused on the darkness outside, avoiding his face. The air was heavy with silence until his ragged sigh broke the stillness.

"Laine, please just say it. What's wrong?"

What could she tell him? If he were plotting against her, she'd make herself even more vulnerable. But if not, then he'd hurt her anyway with the truth about Pat.

"Laine?"

"You're lying to me, Jeff. One way or the other, you've been lying to me."

"Lying? How?"

Though he spoke calmly, she sensed concern in his voice. "I was at the mall yesterday and passed the coffee shop."

In the silence, she heard his intake of breath. "Oh."

She waited, wanting to look at him but afraid of what she'd see.

"I wish you hadn't seen us. It makes things more difficult."

His words pierced her like a dart. "Yes, truth is difficult when you've lived a lie."

"But it's not the lie you expect, Laine. I'm sure of it."

Piqued by curiosity, she lifted her eyes to his, a mixture of anger and confusion. "What does that mean?"

"It means you think I'm having a relationship of some kind with her. A secret romance."

"That's one possibility."

His head drew back, and he appeared to stop himself from moving toward her. "No, no. You don't think I'm involved in this terrible situation, do you? The break-in or plans to hurt you or Becca? I love you, Laine. You and Becca. I love you with all my heart."

She peered at him, swirling in her confusion and doubt. Beware, her mind told her. Con men are smart. They can beguile you to believe anything. "You love me? Come on, Jeff. I might be gullible and naive, but I'm not stupid. Too many things are involved here. I'm not a—"

Before she could stop him, he was on his knees at her feet.

"Yes, I love you. I love you both. It's a long story, and to tell you is a breech of my job and dangerous for you."

"Troubleshooting computers?" she questioned in frustration. Tears rolled down her cheeks. She could take no more.

"No, I'm an undercover cop, Laine. I had to lie to you. Especially now that I find you're involved."

"Me? What? This burglary? Please, don't confuse me."

He took both her hands in his, kissing her fingers. "I don't want to give you details now. We're so close to the end of the investigation. How would I know that you'd move next door to me, and I'd be getting into the situation from both sides?"

"What does that mean?"

"Because I must be sensible and calm. But I care so much about you and Becca, I'm having a difficult time keeping my feelings under control. I want to go wild and do things that could endanger the investigation and your lives. Trust me for now, Laine. I've told you all I can."

His words stuck in her brain like scattered pieces of a puzzle. Was he telling her the truth? She wanted with all her heart to believe him. "But you lied to me. Now you're telling me you're a policeman?"

"Yes, I work undercover. I'm sorry, Laine, but I couldn't tell you."

"But if you're really a policeman, I should have realized."

"Think. Have you noticed that both times when you called the police, I left. Didn't you wonder why? I didn't want any of them to give away my cover accidentally. I was out last night, not troubleshooting computers. I was working on the case. It's not just local anymore. The FBI is involved. The situation's big and dangerous."

Could he be making this up? She couldn't imagine it. "But what about Pat? Who is she?"

"I can't give you details, Laine. And I really didn't know at first who she was. Remember when I slipped up? I nearly gave myself away saying I could investigate her. But she's not your enemy. Can you trust me?"

Could she? She stared at him. "I turned both your names into the police last night." Her heart pounded with the thought.

"You did what?" His eyes narrowed, and he peered at her. "Explain."

"I got a note yesterday—pushed under the screen door there." She pointed to the spot. "Becca found it."

"What kind of note? Why didn't you tell me?"

"Because for all I knew, you wrote it. It said something about Becca and me knowing where the diamonds are and that we can't hide them for much longer."

His face paled. "Dear Lord, no." He closed his eyes as if in prayer. "What did you do?"

"I turned it over to the police and told them my suspicions."

"And I was your suspicion?"

"Not exactly. I'd first thought of Scott Derian. Then the officer asked me what my second thought was. I avoided the questions, but he pressured me. Then I told him about you and Pat."

"They'll have ruled us out, I'm sure, once they realized who we are."

He opened his arms to her and guided her from the chair. "Oh, Laine, you've been so frightened. I'm sorry. I wanted to tell you, but I couldn't. And I can't."

She believed him, maybe foolishly, but she did. She fell into his arms, feeling all the fear and loneliness drain from her. In his arms was where she longed to be. He held her close, his chest pounding against her beating heart.

Then he tilted her chin with his finger and lowered his lips to hers. "You heard me earlier, Laine. I'd wanted to say it at a better moment, but I mean it with all my heart. I love you and Becca. You're precious to me."

"I love you too, Jeff. But I was so hurt and confused."

"You don't have to tell me. I understand."

For a long time, they stayed in each other's arms in silence except for the lapping of the water against the wooden dock and the pulsing of their hearts.

After Jeff went home, Laine crawled into bed, and with light streaking the edge of the horizon, her eyelids finally closed. When the alarm rang, she pried herself from bed, dragging her tired body into the shower.

Once Mavis arrived, Laine explained about the missing Penny, knowing it would be the first thing on Becca's mind. She sneaked in and kissed the sleeping girl on the cheek, then hurried off to work.

Worried about the note and the youngster, she called home later that morning. "Is Becca okay?"

"She's moping around," Mavis said. "I think she's tired, but she's whining about Penny too."

"The doll wasn't at Jeff's?" Laine frowned, wondering where it had gotten to.

"I don't know. It may be there, but he was gone before I called."

"Well, tell her we'll be sure and get her later after he gets home."

"Don't worry," Mavis assured her. "We're fine here."

Laine disconnected, wishing somehow she could erase the preceding days and begin again. Somewhere in the past hours, truth had hung before her like a fragile cord, and she wanted to grab on to it without breaking it. She wanted to bind it to her and cling to a shred of what her life had been like before all the fear and secrets began.

&

Jeff struggled the night away, thinking of the hurt he'd caused Laine. As he reviewed the situation, he ached thinking that for awhile she'd feared him. Yet why wouldn't she after seeing him with Pat? With the pace at which events were taking place, the other secrets he'd kept from her would soon come into the open as well, but he worried that by explaining about Pat's role before everything was resolved, he had put Laine at risk.

He had to be careful. If Laine figured out too much too soon, she and Becca could be placed in real danger. He was on Darren Scott's tail, and that had to be his priority. When Pat laid out her part of the investigation, things fell into place. He was a cop. How could he have been so ignorant?

He rose before the sun, and after draining a pot of coffee and mulling over his thoughts, he dressed and left for the police station. At last the department was getting somewhere, and the sooner the better.

In the briefing room, he sat with other members of the investigation team working on the Scott case and listened to the briefing. Scott Derian. Darren Scott. Why hadn't he caught on earlier? The two men had to be one and the same.

Over the years, Scott had conned Kathleen and other rich widows out of money and gems. The con had begun as common larceny—fraud—but somehow Scott had also gotten involved in the purchase and sale of illegal drugs. What had started simply as an investigation into a larceny complaint had led to the discovery of a drug-trafficking operation that spilled out across state lines, and therefore required the involvement of the FBI.

The detective leaned back in his chair and lit a cigarette. "From the bureau source, we know Scott's feeling the pinch and running scared. He's blown his cover, but we can't pick him up yet. We've got the suppliers at our fingertips, and that's what we're waiting for. Scott's going to make his move. Then we get 'em both—Scott and the drug suppliers."

Jeff scowled. "What do you mean, 'He's running scared'?" His thoughts raced to Laine and Becca's safety.

"Promises he can't keep. He's getting sloppy. We know he's been hanging around the Sibley place. He left a note there yesterday. The FBI agent sees two possibilities. He either knows for sure Kathleen Keary had more wealth hidden, or he's picked up on the wealthy grandmother. Whichever is the case, he's obviously out for more. And he's scratching the bottom of the barrel to cover his drug debts. He's desperate."

"Desperate? So what are we doing about it?" Jeff asked, attempting to appear calm. Hearing the detective use words like "running scared" and "desperate," his pulse had already kicked into full gear.

"Don't panic. We're on it. After the break-in, we put on surveillance 'round the clock."

"Surveillance? We can do more than that!"

"Look, you know the routine. We need the names of

Scott's contacts, and then we need to catch him in the act. Hard evidence. We can't bring him in until we have both. Scott's con game is chicken feed. The drug suppliers are our meat and potatoes."

Jeff closed his eyes. Chicken feed? No way. When it came to Laine and Becca's safety, the con wasn't a game or chicken feed. He knew he had to stay cool and in control, but a man like Scott, afraid for his life, acted out of desperation. He wouldn't care whom he hurt. And the people he could hurt included people Jeff loved. If Darren Scott was heading for Laine's, he had to do something.

Jeff thought of what Pat Sabin had told him. He remembered how shocked he'd been to learn Pat was an undercover FBI agent. Using the last name "Sorrento," she'd befriended Kathleen to get closer to Scott Derian. Through that friendship, she'd been able to keep an eye on his con game and gather information for the bureau.

But her mission had backfired. Pat had been touched by Kathleen and Becca, especially after witnessing their struggle following Kathleen's illness and death, and Pat had fought her emotional involvement, recognizing that she couldn't allow her friendship to get in the way of the investigation.

Jeff understood her problem. Laine and Becca could easily get in his way. But he couldn't interfere. The police chief assigned his job. Surveillance was someone else's responsibility. If he botched this, someone could get hurt. And that someone could be Laine.

He wrestled with his fears. The people running this job knew what was best—or did they?

☙

Concentrating was nearly impossible for Laine. Over the past few weeks, focusing on a new firm, new clients, and new designs had become nearly impossible. It was time to face her decision about Becca's future head on. She had to talk to Glynnis and explain everything. Even the thought, uttered in the silence of her mind, bored through her nerves like a dentist's drill. The pain was too deep and too excruciating to bear.

For her problem was no longer simply concern over Becca's future. The anonymous note she had received told her the present could be dangerous as well. Jeff had given her hope. The police were closing in, but until they were all safe, she couldn't let down her guard.

Strangely, the tribulations that kept pouring through her life had led her back to her faith—not a perfect faith, but a beginning. But why when she had turned back to God, back to her Savior, did He allow new fears and worries to enter her life? Was it a test? A trial of some kind? What more could happen to measure her endurance?

When the telephone rang at three in the afternoon, she sat unmoving. Fear rose in her, a cold, icy terror like the feeling that follows the call announcing a loved one has died. She lifted the telephone, barely able to understand Mavis's frantic message.

"What are you saying, Mavis? I can't understand you." Laine's pulse roared in her ears.

"Becca," Mavis repeated. "She's gone."

Laine's heart stood still. "Becca? Gone? Where? What are you talking about?" Her limbs trembled, shaking out of control.

"I don't know. First, I heard a woman's voice and Becca's laugh. Then I heard a car drive off. She's gone."

"A woman's voice? Did you see her? What did she say?"

"I heard her say, 'Hi there, Kiddo.' I headed for the door,

but she was already gone."

Kiddo. Pat. Laine's heart pounded, hammered like a war drum. "Call the police, Mavis. Tell them Pat Sorrento kidnaped Becca. I'm leaving now."

She slammed the telephone on the receiver and darted from her office. Job, no job. She didn't care. She had to find Becca. She trusted Jeff, and he'd told her Pat wasn't her enemy. But why did the woman take Becca? Why?

Jeff. She needed Jeff, and she needed him now.

thirteen

When the surveillance call came in that Darren Scott, alias Scott Derian, had made his move, Jeff knew Becca was safe. Pat had taken her away before any danger might come to her. Mavis, hopefully, could take care of herself, but they needed to protect the child. Pat warned the department of Darren Scott's kidnapping plan. With Becca's abduction, he could demand money from Glynnis or the missing fortune he seemed to think Kathleen had hidden from him, or both.

Now with Becca in safety, the police were closing in on Scott. With the goods on him for the first breaking and entering, along with the other attempted B and Es and kidnapping, they had him where they wanted him.

Pat Sabin had provided the key. After Scott split with Kathleen's property, she'd made contact with him, threatening to turn him in to the police unless he took her in as a partner. For a share of the take, she offered to be his liaison with other rich widows whom she would befriend, setting him up for another con job, and she worked her way into Scott's confidence. Over the months, she learned where he stashed his stolen cash and jewelry. Once the heat was off, he would sell the gems to a fence, then use the cash to foot his drug business. But this time, they had cornered him red-handed.

And most important, the department figured he'd squeal and turn state's evidence if they offered him a plea bargain. Scott was a small boat in a large sea. And they were headed for the luxury liner—the drug-trafficking kingpin.

Though Becca was safe, Jeff feared for Laine and Mrs. Dexter. Knowing the police were on their way to nab Scott, Jeff raced toward the condo as fast as his unmarked car allowed.

≈

Laine's heart thundered in her ears as she tore into the driveway. No squad car. The police should have arrived by now. Then she caught sight of an unmarked car standing cockeyed at the curb in front of the condo as if someone had barreled up and rushed into the house. A detective, she prayed.

She bolted from the car and snatched open the back door, her pulse racing. Fear tore through every nerve. "Mavis!" she yelled. Before she could take in the scene in the kitchen, someone grabbed hold of her shoulder. Jerking her around, a stranger glared at her, his eyes narrowed and his mouth pinched in anger.

"Who are you?" the man bellowed.

In confusion, she glanced around the room and saw Mavis cowering against the wall across from her, terror written on her face. "Laine Sibley," she said in a whisper. "What are you doing here?"

"Shut your mouth," he barked. "I'm asking the questions." He jammed her against the wall, pinning her by the throat. He snarled into her face. "Where's the kid?"

She tried to speak, but the pressure of his powerful hand choked off the sound.

"I told you," Mavis said, her voice wavering with fright. "She's been kidnapped."

He shifted toward her and snarled. "Shut up, you old hag. You don't know what you're talking about."

He released his grip a fraction, and Laine coughed, trying to find her voice. "Really," Laine gasped. "Someone took her. A woman. What do you want with her?" Tears blurred her vision.

He glared at her, lowering his red, glazed eyes until they were nose to nose. The veins pulsated in his temples, and his jaw muscles flexed like a tic as he growled into her face, "A woman? You think I'm a fool?"

Laine turned her head, avoiding his crazed eyes.

He jabbed at her again, sliding his hand toward her throat. "Do you think I'm a fool?" he thundered again.

"It's true. A woman," Laine rasped. "Pat Sorrento." She choked out her name.

He flinched as if he'd been hit with a mallet. A sneer covered his face. "That dirty double-crosser," he screamed. "I'll kill her."

He released Laine with a vicious shove and spun toward the door. Before he had one foot on the porch, a police officer spun him around and yanked his hands behind his back. Noise rose from the yard. Laine cringed against the wall as the shouts and clamor continued. She noticed that Mavis had crumpled into a chair and sat with her face in her hands. As Laine turned toward the elderly woman, a commotion sounded outside the door.

୬

Jeff sped into the kitchen, fearful of what he might find. As soon as he saw Laine, he drew her into his arms. Both Laine and Mrs. Dexter looked ashen and shaken but unharmed, and a ragged breath tore from him as Laine's quaking body clung to him.

"Are you all right?" he asked, burying his face in her hair to hide his own trembling fear.

She nodded, and in her swallowed sobs, she questioned him. "Becca?" She lifted her tear-filled eyes to his.

"Becca's okay. Don't worry. They didn't have time to call you. I'm sorry."

"But where is she?"

"She's with Pat."

A bewildered look filled her eyes. "I knew it was Pat. Remember when I told you I had a strange feeling about her." Covering her face with her hands, she paused, then wiped her eyes. "But why did she take her?"

"To keep her safe. Pat Sabin's with the FBI, Laine. They wanted her out of the way when they knew Scott was heading here. It was the best thing they could do. Pat and Becca are probably somewhere having an ice-cream cone."

"Ice cream? Pat Sabin?" Laine looked confused.

"Sabin's her real name."

"It's all too confusing." She buried her head on his shoulder, her tears soaking through his shirt.

"Pat'll bring Becca home soon," he said, hoping to calm her. "She'll check with the station to make sure the danger's past. Becca's fine."

He turned his attention to Mrs. Dexter. "Are you okay?" His question seemed foolish as he stared into the elderly woman's death-white face.

Mavis gaped at him with a dazed expression and mumbled with quivering lips, "I don't understand. What did the man want? He asked for Becca."

"Scott Derian planned to kidnap Becca, hoping to get some more money. . .either from Glynnis or from you, Laine."

"Me?" She stared up at him. "I don't have anything."

"He apparently thinks you know where the rest of Kathleen's jewels and money are."

"But I don't know anything. For all I know, he took it all."

He nestled her to his chest. "Well, Scott thinks you do."

"That evil man was Scott Derian?"

Jeff nodded.

"I. . .we were so frightened, Jeff." She lifted her desperate, tear-filled eyes to his.

"I know." He caressed her golden hair, soothing her fears as best he could but concerned by how weak she felt in his arms. "You need to sit, Laine." He grabbed a chair that had toppled to the floor and set it upright, then eased Laine down next to Mrs. Dexter. Crouching beside her, Jeff patted her tensed arm. "Were you home when he got here?"

"No." She shook her head. "Just Mavis, I guess."

The woman peered at them with a look of amazement on her pale face as if she only then realized what had happened. She sighed weakly.

"It must have been terrible," Laine said, her voice filled with sadness. "What happened before I came?"

Before Mavis could answer, a rap on the back screen door drew their attention. An officer stepped into the kitchen. "I need to finish this report, Jeff. Okay?"

"Sure," he said, rising from his crouched position next to Laine. "We'd just asked Mrs. Dexter what happened. She was here alone when Scott got here."

The officer lifted the clipboard and stepped closer to Mavis. "Ma'am, what's your name and your relationship to the Sibley family?"

She lifted her eyes to his. "Mavis. Mavis Dexter. I sit with Becca. . .Rebecca, Miss Sibley's niece."

He scribbled on the form. "Ma'am, could you tell me what happened as best you can remember?"

"I'm not really sure what happened myself," Mavis said, her voice still unsteady. She closed her eyes as if trying to recall the event. "After I talked to Laine, that's Miss Sibley, on the phone, I did what she said and called the police. I've never been so frightened in my life."

The elderly woman looked so shaken, Jeff walked to her side and rested his hand on her shoulder.

She looked at him with a thankful gaze before she continued. "So I hurried to the kitchen door, waiting for the police, but when a car pulled up, I was confused for a minute because it wasn't marked. A man rushed to the door, and like a fool I opened it. I thought it was a detective—you know, like the TV programs."

"You're not a fool, Mrs. Dexter. That made sense." Jeff's empathy rose for the distressed woman.

Her hands still trembled as she nestled them in her lap. "But instead of saying anything, he jerked the door open and pushed me against the wall. Then he demanded to see the kid. That's what he called Becca."

"Oh, I'm so sorry, Mavis," Laine sympathized. "Did he hurt you?"

"No, no, he just knocked me against the wall, like he did you. I told him she was gone. . .kidnapped, but before I could say anything else, you burst in."

The officer turned to Laine. "Could you fill me in on what happened next?"

Laine told him about Mavis's phone call and what happened as she came into the kitchen. As she recalled the event, she slowed and turned to Jeff. "Scott knew Pat? But I don't understand."

"He thought Pat was working for him," Jeff said. "I'll explain later."

She stared at him for a moment, then turned again to the officer. "I guess that was it. When he ran out, you were there. You know the rest," she said to the young man.

The officer ran through the report, verifying the facts, and then walked back outside.

Jeff watched him as he left. "Let's go into the living room where it's more comfortable. You and Mavis can relax and talk. I'll make you a cup of something—tea or coffee. You need to calm yourselves."

Laine didn't argue, so he took her arm, helping her from the chair, then helped Mavis to stand up. When the two women were settled in the living room, he turned on the tea-kettle returned to the backyard. The officers were finishing, and when the last car finally pulled away, Jeff returned to the kitchen.

As the kettle whistled, Becca's voice sounded in the yard. Chattering merrily with Pat, she bounded into the kitchen. "Aunt Pat took me for ice cream. And while we were gone, the police came and caught a bad guy. Did you know that?"

"I sure did," he said, tousling her hair. "You'd better go give your aunt Laine and Mrs. Dexter a hug. They were worried about you."

"I know." She hung her head. "Aunt Pat wouldn't let me come in and tell Mrs. Dexter. She said we had to hurry."

As she skipped out of the room, Pat gaped at him. "That kid is a smart one. Even knowing me and with the promise of ice cream, she cried when I made her come along without telling Mrs. Dexter. If I'd been a stranger, she'd have kicked and bitten, I'm sure."

"Good for her," Jeff said, grinning. "And thanks for all your help. I'm glad this thing is over, and I can go back to being me. And get rid of this beard."

"She'll like you either way," Pat grinned, tilting her head toward the living room. "I'm almost jealous."

"Sure you are."

Pat gave him a wink and edged toward the door. "Listen, before she hits me with a frying pan, I'm going to squeak out of here. You can explain everything. I have reports to do."

"I'd say, 'It's been nice,' but . . ."

"No need. So long." She gave him a wave.

When she was gone, he finished the tea and carried a tray into the living room.

Laine looked up, her eyes filled with unspoken questions. Becca nestled in her arm, and Mavis, as white as a new dress shirt, leaned against the chair back as if she were still trying to figure things out.

He handed them each a cup of tea and set the creamer and sugar bowl down between them, then slid onto the sofa beside Laine. "Hope the tea helps. You both look pale—to say the least."

Unexpectedly, Becca turned and faced Jeff. "Do you know where Penny is? She's been gone the whole night and day."

"I think she's at my house, Becca. Sorry I forgot to bring her home." He tweaked her cheek tenderly.

"Can I get her?" She looked at Jeff, then turned to Laine.

"She's right on my porch, and the screen door's unlocked, I think."

Becca eyed Laine for permission.

An uneasy feeling shivered through Laine. "I don't know." She gave Jeff a questioning look.

"It's over, Laine. I'll keep my eye on her. Nothing can happen. . .now."

She studied his face to feel secure with his response, then turned to Becca. "Go ahead, Sweetie. But if the screen's locked, hurry back, and Jeff will go with you."

Becca raced out the door, and Jeff stood up to watch the child's progress.

Laine looked up at Jeff. "Since Becca's gone for a second, can you explain some of this mess to me?"

He glanced down at her with an understanding grin. "I noticed you were ready to burst with questions."

Jeff filled them in, speaking as fast as an auctioneer. He offered enough details to explain Darren Scott's plan and Pat's involvement.

Laine glanced at Mavis, seeing confusion linger in the woman's eyes. "I know you're confused, Mavis. I'll explain more later when Becca's not around."

Mavis nodded, apparently understanding enough for the moment.

But Laine had one more question she was hesitant to ask. Taking a deep breath, she plunged ahead. "Jeff, Pat Sorrento—Sabin—wasn't really Kathleen's friend?" The thought brought an ache to her heart.

"That's not true, Laine. Pat told me she originally struck up a friendship with Kathleen so she could get closer to Scott. I think they met in a park one day and chatted. Pat placed herself in places she'd run into Kathleen so they could form a friendship. But in time she became really fond of both Kathleen and Becca. She said she tried to drop hints about Scott without endangering the investigation."

"I wonder if she listened. I suppose that part doesn't matter. I'm glad, Jeff. I'm glad Kathleen had a real friend."

Laine rose and wandered to Jeff's side, then ran her fingers along Jeff's beard. "So are you going to tell me this is part of your masquerade?"

He nodded. "Afraid it is. Something to hide under so I looked a little different. By the way, there's another small surprise."

She waited for the blow, wondering what other pretenses she'd believed.

Jeff turned toward her. "My name isn't Jeff Rice."

"Don't tell me it's Stanley or Aloysius. I'm calling you Jeff, regardless."

"Good. The Jeff part's right. My last name's Reese."

"So you're telling me I have to get to know a beardless man named Jeff Reese?"

"Have to? I hope you want to. He's nearly the same nice guy as that Mr. Rice you're always talking about. The guy who loves you."

Mavis looked at them both with a grin. "Sounds like I should leave and let you two get to know each other. . .alone."

Laine shook her head. "We're rarely alone, Mavis. Have you ever tried to have a moment of privacy with Becca around? It's impossible."

"Now that you mention it. . ." Mavis chuckled.

Thinking of Becca, both Laine and Jeff turned to look out at his yard. When she glanced back at him, she saw the same question in his eyes that she knew was in her own. "Where is she?" Laine asked, concern edging into her voice.

"I was watching. . .until I got distracted," Jeff said. "But she's okay. She has to be."

He darted toward the doorway. "I'll check and be right back," he called over his shoulder as he tore outside.

"I'll come too," Laine called, bolting after him. Mavis followed, peering through the screen door.

Laine caught up to Jeff as he checked his front porch from the top step. He jerked the door open and called Becca's name, but no answer came. He tested the front door, but it was locked.

Clinging to the doorjamb, Laine's free hand clenched against her chest to calm her pounding heart. "Where could she be?"

"She has to be here somewhere," Jeff answered, striding

past Laine to the outside again. She followed him to the edge of the condo, and as they turned the corner of the building, both stopped and then turned to each other in relief. Though their hearts pounded, laughter rose from their throats.

Becca sat on the ground totally lost in her activity, Penny lying neglected on the ground beside her. In Becca's lap, a small, furry calico kitten clambered up her chest, scraping kisses on her hand with its sandpaper tongue as she tried to pet the excited creature. She nuzzled the kitten against her cheek, then caught their gaze. Jumping up, Becca darted toward them with the squirming fur ball in her arms. "Look, Auntie. A kitten."

"Becca, you scared us to death," Laine said, a scowl and grin fighting for a place on her face.

"But look, a kitty." Becca jutted the kitten toward Laine. Her voice piped with excitement. "Can I keep it?"

Jeff chuckled with amusement. "Let's see you get out of this one, Auntie," he whispered.

Laine raised her eyebrow toward him and spoke to Becca. "You didn't listen to me, Becca. You should never scare me like this again. You were supposed to come right back."

"I know, but the kitty ran around the corner, and I forgot." Her eyes lifted to Laine's, pleading. "Auntie, I really love this kitty."

Laine swallowed the emotion rising in her throat. "I'm sure you do." Becca's words struck her heart with more meaning than she could say. Laine knew about love. She loved Jeff, and she loved Becca with her whole heart. She gave Becca a quick hug. "If we find out the kitty doesn't belong to someone else, then we can keep it."

❧

Laine sat alone and recalled the events of the past days. If nothing else, the horrible incidents made one thing very clear: She knew what she had to do. Becca meant more to her than anything in the world. She had to convince Glynnis that the child should remain here with her.

Later that evening when Jeff returned, she described her feelings to him. In a rare moment of privacy, they nestled on the porch while a gentle breeze wafted through the screens. Laine described her mental struggle—the pros, the cons, and the in-betweens of keeping custody of Becca.

"I realize Glynnis hasn't shared the experience of living day in and day out with Becca, so she may not fully understand what it entails. But I have to make her realize that Becca's place is here. When Mavis called me today and I thought Becca might be hurt or I might lose her, I was overwhelmed with desperation. I've never felt such a loss. Not even with Kathleen. Any child is special. And this child is precious to me." She envisioned the small child, nestled in bed with the tiny fur ball at her side. Laine had been relieved when a neighbor whose cat was the mother of the kitten had given permission for Becca to keep the little animal.

Jeff nuzzled his clean-shaven cheek against her face, and she grinned at him, enjoying the new smooth feeling.

But another thought intruded. She turned to face Jeff. "Having you in my life is wonderful. And if Glynnis listens to me, I'll have Becca in my life and Scott Darian—or whatever his name is—out of it, and everything will be complete." She paused and looked at him. "Except for one more thing. If Scott was so certain Kathleen had something hidden, sure enough to kidnap Becca and to break in here, he must have had some kind of evidence, wouldn't you think?"

"Maybe. But maybe it's wishful thinking. People like him get paranoid when they're in trouble. They imagine anything."

"I suppose." A strange sensation rippled through her. Something told her Scott might be closer to the truth than they were. She sighed and rose, crossing to Jeff as he watched out the screen window. "So hopefully, we can breathe again."

"I think we can all breathe again." He stood behind her and wrapped his arms around her waist.

"I'll call Glynnis tomorrow and pray that God gives me the right words." She turned, looking into Jeff's face. "And you know, besides the daily joy of having Becca here, she's given me something I never expected. The Bible says, 'And a little child shall lead them.' Becca did that. She led me—led both of us, really—back to church and back to reading Scripture and—"

"And prayer. A key to everything."

"And to pray." Her eyes welled up with tears. "What had I done all those years without it?"

Jeff chuckled. "You probably prayed without thinking. I did, despite what I said about my faith."

"Me too, I suppose. I'm sure I did."

"Not wanting to disillusion you, though." He tilted her chin upward.

"What?" Her pulse skipped a beat. Please, God, not another problem. "Tell me."

He chuckled. "Don't look so panicky. I just wanted to remind you that when the Bible said, 'And a little child shall lead them,' it was talking about Jesus, not a regular child. Just a point of fact."

"Did you write the Bible?" She elbowed him playfully.

"No."

"Well then. . .it can have two meanings. I know it means Jesus, but remember, we're to have faith like a child. And Becca was our example. Her faith strengthened ours."

"You win." His arm slid firmly around her back, and he drew her closer.

Her upper body molded against his powerful chest where she felt safe and protected. His lips touched hers with a gentle firmness she could never explain, but one that filled her with completeness.

As they drew apart, a chuckle rose to her lips.

"You're laughing at my kiss?"

"No, I'm remembering when you told me months ago about your work—when I said you seemed more like a Superman than a troubleshooter. You said everything so inside out it didn't make much sense."

"That's because I hated to lie to you even though I had to. So I didn't say I was a computer troubleshooter. Remember? I said I was a troubleshooter. Then I said, computers. You put the two together."

"Oh, right! Blame me. Wish I had a tape recording of that conversation."

"Anyway, you have the truth now."

"I'm glad." She squeezed his hand.

He thought a moment. "Except for one thing. And don't panic." He drew his fingers along her cheek. "But it's something that's troubled me for years—something I couldn't talk about. But now I can, and I'm thankful God heard my prayers and took the guilt-ridden feelings away."

"What?" She tried to imagine what had made him serious again.

"I'd spent the past years wanting revenge, wanting to get even with men like Scott. But since I met you and Becca and you've become so important to me, I wanted to see him captured and punished for your safety and no other reason. You and Becca were all I cared about."

Looking into his eyes, she watched his hurt and sorrow melt to a reassuring calm. "I love you, beardless Jeff Reese —or whoever you are."

"But think of how much fun you'll have getting to know the real me. And remember, no matter who I am, I love you with all my heart."

His lips touched hers again, firmer and surer. And this time she definitely believed every word he said.

fourteen

After church on Sunday, Jeff suggested that he, Laine, and Becca go for a swim. He grinned to himself, his surprise gathering momentum. He reached Laine's dock before she did, and using the rake, he pulled in a few strands of seaweed. He'd worked hard to clear the shallower water so Becca could play without getting tangled in the drifting weeds.

When he heard a giggle, he looked up to see Becca darting from the house with Laine close behind, carrying the towels and a safety vest. The new kitten, still unnamed, skittered behind them. Once she fitted Becca in a vest, Laine joined Jeff sitting on the edge of the dock, and the two adults watched the little girl splash and play in the water. Their talk was casual, but Jeff knew they still had serious issues to handle before they could close the door on their problems.

But the afternoon was special, no matter what lay ahead, and Jeff's heart kept a wilder pace, waiting for the opportune moment. Finally, while Laine was distracted by Becca's antics, he reached in the small key pocket of his swimsuit and pulled out a tiny box. He slid it on the boards between them.

"Okay, Becca, I've watched enough for awhile," Laine said, rolling her eyes at him. "Practice swimming the way I showed you, okay?" She turned her attention to him. "Now," she said, grinning, "we might have one minute."

"One minute, huh?" He slid his hand across her shoulders. "I just found something in my pocket." A secret grin hedged on his lips.

"In your pocket? What?"

He pointed to the tiny box sitting between them.

"What's this?" She stared at the small container. "It could slip through the dock slats if you're not careful." A hint of excitement slipped into her voice.

"Then why don't you pick it up?"

She hesitated and drew the box carefully into her hands. Unmoving, she stared at it.

"So? Open it."

When she lifted the lid, a gasp escaped her. "Jeff, it's a ring. A diamond?" Her eyes widened as she gazed at the stone.

"What else would it be?" He lifted the small ring from the piece of cotton. "I'm asking you to be my—"

The ring slipped from his hand and dropped to the dark cushion of mud beneath the sandy water.

"No!" she wailed. "Becca, don't move, Sweetie. Don't stir up the water."

Laine jumped into the gritty lake, and Jeff's heart lifted, remembering the day they'd first met. When she came to the surface, her lovely peacock-hued eyes were wider than he'd ever seen, and his heart pounded.

"Why are you just sitting there?" she asked, her arms flailing.

He grinned without moving.

"This isn't funny. I can't see the ring at all. It's gone."

"You can get one just like that in any Cracker Jack box in town."

Noticeably confused, she peered at him, her face shifting to a scowl. "What are you talking about?"

He gestured. "It's not the real thing like the one in my pocket."

She shook her head with a frown and smacked the water in

exasperation. "You! I can't believe you! Why did you do that?"

"I'm just a romantic. Remember how we met? You looked so beautiful and so funny when you bobbed up out of the water. I just had to see you again with that surprised look on your face." He rose and hoisted her to the dock, his arms slipping around her wet, dripping body.

In playful frustration, she pounded his broad chest with her fists. "You're terrible. You scared me."

"I know, but it was worth the look on your face."

"You are an absolute tease."

He spread a towel on the boards, and this time when they sat, he brought out a ring that glinted like blue fire. He slipped it on her finger and kissed her hand. "For better or worse," he asked, "will you marry me?"

"After that dirty trick, I should say no, but I'm no fool. Yes. Yes. Yes."

Becca, watching curiously, paddled to the edge of the dock. "Me too," Becca said, joining the enthusiasm. "Yes. Yes."

"What, Angel? You want to marry me too?" Jeff asked.

"Uh-huh, me and Penny."

"Okay, then I guess it's a threesome. . .or foursome." He wiggled his eyebrows at her, and she giggled.

"Watch me," she called and paddled along the shoreline for a couple of feet.

Jeff turned to Laine. "You can see how much I impress the girls. I just agreed to marry her, and all she wants to do is swim away."

"But I hope you've noticed I'm not going anywhere," Laine said, offering him her eager, waiting lips.

&

Laine sat with her hand still clinging to the telephone. She'd waited as long as she could to face Glynnis with her decision, but time had run out. She'd just arranged for the two of them and Jeff to meet that afternoon.

She glanced at her lovely diamond shimmering in the afternoon light. God's hand had guided her life this far even when she had turned her back on Him. The Lord didn't let His children slip too far before His gracious hand lifted them up again and set them on their feet.

So many of her problems had dissipated; her guilt had disappeared when she understood repentance and asked for forgiveness.

Now her loneliness vanished having Becca and Jeff at her side, and her sorrow faded knowing Kathleen's faith had been strong. With Scott Derian—or Darren Scott—out of her life, they were again safe and secure. Her final meeting with Glynnis would finalize it all—except for Kathleen's inheritance. And perhaps she would never know what had happened to those jewels.

Laine uncoiled her fingers from the telephone receiver and walked to the living-room window. Becca sat on the porch, sounding out a storybook to the kitten, who cuddled on her lap.

"You're reading some pretty big words, Becca."

The girl grinned at Laine through the window. "I have to be smart in school. So I'm practicing."

"Good for you." She gazed at her sister's lovely child, who had inherited Alex's Irish coloring, fair skin and dark hair with the bluest eyes. It was time to prepare her, let her know what the day held. . .just in case. Most of all, she needed to know what Becca wanted.

Laine wandered out to the porch and sat on the wicker love seat, watching the child for a few moments before she disquieted her play with questions.

"Becca?"

Becca paused in midsentence, the storybook suspended in front of her.

"Would you come here for a minute so we can talk?" Laine asked.

Her eyes brightened. Without question, she set the book on the side table and the kitten on the floor, then slipped into the seat beside Laine.

Laine kissed her cheek. "I'm going to visit your grandmother this afternoon to talk about you."

"Me?" Becca's curious eyes gazed up at Laine.

"Uh-huh. I'll drop you off at Mrs. Dexter's for awhile. Your grandma and I have some important decisions to make. But I'd like to know how you feel too."

Becca gazed at her without saying a word, listening intently.

"School starts in a few days, and I've waited too long to get you registered. But before that, I have to know which school you'll be going to. Your grandma and I would both like to have you live with us, but you know that's impossible."

She nodded her head matter-of-factly.

"You can visit with both of us. But you have to live in one spot." With her heart thudding in her throat, Laine looked at the child.

"I already live with you, Auntie."

Her answer was simple. "Yes, you do now, but your grandma can give you more things and lots more time than I have. I go to work every day and—"

"And Mrs. Dexter stays with me."

Laine remembered Becca's decisive choices when they shopped for school clothes. The child clearly knew what she wanted. "That's right." She held her breath. "Is that the way you want it to be? Your grandma loves you very much, and she'd like you to live with her too."

A sudden silence filled the room, a rare silence in Becca's case. For a long time, she looked out toward the water. No emotion—no fear or confusion—etched her dainty face, only serious thought. Slowly, she turned to Laine. "My mommy always said I should love my grandma. But I never saw her. Now, you take me to see her, and I love my grandma."

"I know you do, Sweetheart." Laine's chest ached from her halting breath.

"I want to see my grandma for visits. I live with you."

A ragged sigh escaped Laine. "And that's the way you want it? You're sure?"

"Uh-huh. My mommy said if she couldn't watch me, you would take care of me."

"Your mom told you that?" Laine peered at her upturned face. "When did she say that?"

"She always said it. She said you loved me."

Laine nestled the child in her arm, fighting the tears that pushed against her eyes. "Your mommy was right. I love you with all my heart."

"And I take care of Penny like you take care of me."

"You sure do." A new awareness washed over her. She'd worried about Becca's preoccupation with the raggedy doll. Now she understood where it came from. Kathleen must have used the doll as an example.

"Then when I see your grandma today, I'll let her know that this is what you want. I hope she listens to me."

"She will, Auntie. I already told her I wanted to live with you."

Laine closed her eyes, unbelieving. "You did?"

"Uh-huh. Grandma asked me if I could live anyplace in the world, where did I want to live. I said with you."

Laine couldn't speak from the force of the love that

pressed against her heart.

❧

Jeff parked the car and glanced at Laine. Though nervous, her eyes were glowing and confident. She'd made her decision about Becca based on every logical piece of evidence she had. Kathleen had willed it, Becca wanted it, and Laine longed and prayed for it. God's will would be done.

He slid from the car, and before he reached Laine's door, she had already stepped to the ground. He took her arm and guided her up the brick steps to the wide, elegant doorway. He'd seen the outside of the huge dwelling before but had never been inside. He and Glynnis had met only a few times while transporting Becca from house to house.

The door opened, and to his surprise, Glynnis greeted them. She too, appeared confident and collected. They stepped inside, and he gaped at the impressive foyer. Wide solid-oak baseboards and doorframes glistened with varnish and years of polish. Thick plastered walls met a coved ceiling ten to twelve feet above the floor, and a glimmering crystal chandelier glinted in the afternoon light.

Glynnis led them to a wide, deep living room graced by a stone fireplace and heavy brocade furniture. Opulence and wealth spoke out at every turn.

When they were seated, Laine's words lifted from her with grace and ease, and his heart soared to hear her address the elderly woman with her new confidence.

"First, I want to share some wonderful news." Laine extended her hand. "Jeff and I are engaged. We'll be married before Christmas. We've known each other only a few months, but sometimes God's voice rings loud and clear. And I know this is meant to be."

Glynnis took her hand and gazed down at the diamond

glinting shards of blue and red fire. "It's lovely. Truly lovely. Congratulations to both of you."

Laine folded her hands in her lap and breathed deeply. "As I said, God's voice sometimes speaks clearly. I've done a lot of Bible reading since Kathleen's death and Becca's arrival. The other day I read a verse that had so much meaning for me I was nearly dumbfounded."

He watched amazed as she pulled the small white Testament from her handbag and opened it to a marked page.

She lifted her eyes to Glynnis. "It's from Philippians, chapter four: 'I know what it is to be in need, and I know what it is to have plenty. I have learned the secret of being content in any and every situation, whether well fed or hungry, whether living in plenty or in want. I can do everything through Him who gives me strength.' "

Jeff studied her when she finished reading. She placed her hands in her lap and sat in silence, the only sound being the even ticking of the grandfather clock beating in rhythm with their hearts.

"I'm not sure if either of you understands what I'm hearing in God's Word, but I'll try to explain. In my early years I struggled for every penny I earned. But worse, most of my life I felt starved for love, hungry for affection, needing someone's accolades. Recently, God's given me those things through Jeff and Becca, but I learned something from these two important people. I learned the secret of being content. It's within me—not something on the outside that I can get from something or someone but inside. It has to do with faith."

She looked at both of them as if searching their eyes for understanding.

"Glynnis, when I first came here, I thought you had so

much more to give Becca than I do. You have wealth, status, breeding, so many opportunities that I might not be able to give her. But I've learned that those aren't what makes a person rich. It's knowing God's grace and salvation. It's understanding forgiveness, and it's knowing, no matter how little or how much you have, God loves you. Becca knows Jesus' love—and I'm thankful that she knows we all love her too. I believe that—"

"Laine." Glynnis leaned forward, looking earnestly into the younger woman's face. "Thank you for sharing your beliefs with me. But I made up my mind a few weeks ago where Rebecca belongs."

Laine clasped her hand to her chest, tears brimming her eyes.

"She belongs with you. It's where her mother wanted her, and it's where she'll have all the things she needs. I love her, yes, and my money is still hers. I've created a trust fund for her so she can have all the education and travel she'll want someday. But her home is with you."

Laine lifted her hands and covered her eyes, tears rolling from beneath her fingers. "Thank you, Glynnis. Thank you for understanding."

"I asked Rebecca awhile ago where she wanted to live, and she said with you. And one thing Rebecca inherited from her father was decisiveness. She knows what she wants." The elderly woman smiled at them. "It's the best and most appropriate place for her to be."

Through her tears, Laine smiled. "Just to be honest with you, I asked her too. She said the same thing. But thank you for respecting her wishes."

Jeff drew a ragged breath. If he didn't do something soon, he'd be wiping away his own tears. "All right then, I have an idea. Tomorrow we'll celebrate. Let's have dinner together to show Becca we're all in agreement." He looked at the two women's pleased expressions and accepted their silence as agreement.

fifteen

On the way to dinner, Laine silently thanked God for answering her prayers. Her eyes searched the sky, knowing God looked down on her, and she wondered if He was smiling at her, seeing that His love and mercy had formed the plan for Becca's care long before they could ever imagine.

Jeff took them to a lovely restaurant that Glynnis graciously observed was excellent. Laine smiled when Jeff suggested going back to the house for dessert and coffee. She understood. Glynnis had never been inside the house, never seen where Becca lived. It was time.

With their simple dessert eaten, they sat on Laine's screened porch, sipping coffee and watching the setting sun provide a spectacular display for their celebration. Streamers of deep orange, copper, and magenta swept across the horizon with wisps of cerulean blue and deep pink running like dye from the wash of color. Glynnis gave repeated oohs and aahs as she enjoyed the stunning display.

Kitty gravitated to Glynnis's feet until the woman grasped the kitten in her hand and lifted it to her lap. "My, my, little kitten, you do want attention."

"Kitty loves you, Grandma," Becca said, "just like I do."

Glynnis's face flashed with a quick succession of emotions. Becca's words had obviously touched her. "And I love you too. . .and your kitten." She held the cat up, eye-level. "And what is this tiny creature called?" She lowered her gaze to Becca.

"Just Kitty. It doesn't have a name yet," Becca said with a giggle. "But let's give it one, Grandma."

Despite her exuberance, Becca quieted, looking quizzically at the kitten for a moment. "Is it a boy or girl?"

Glynnis looked at her tenderly and tipped the kitten upside down, then grinned. "I'd say this one is a bonnie lass."

"Bonnie lass," Becca repeated. "That's what we'll call her."

"Well, Dear," Glynnis said, "I think Bonnie would be quite enough."

"Sounds like a good name to me," Jeff agreed.

Laine swallowed back the joy that surged through her, watching the child and her grandmother.

Becca slid the kitten from her grandmother's grasp and wrapped Bonnie in her arms.

The conversation turned to other topics, and as the time neared for Glynnis to return home, Becca slid onto her lap with the poor forgotten Penny snagged under her arm. The overloved Bonnie had defensively curled into a ball and slept in the corner of the sofa.

Glynnis wrapped an arm around Becca and eyed the pitiful doll with a sigh. "I guess my efforts were useless." She slipped the doll from Becca's hand and held the toy in front of her. "I don't quite see the charm, I'm afraid. You like this doll best, though, don't you, Rebecca?"

Embarrassed at Becca's disinterest in the lovely doll that Glynnis had given, Laine began to explain the child's preoccupation with Penny, but she'd only begun when Becca took over.

"My mommy told me to take good care of Penny, Grandma. So I do. Mommy said Penny was precious. When she got torn, she sewed her up for me."

Jeff touched Laine's arm. "Your mommy sewed up your doll?" He looked intently at Laine.

Laine's heart skipped a beat. "How did she get torn?" she asked her niece.

Heaving a great sigh, Becca looked at her. "I don't know, but Mommy said she got ripped."

"What do you think?" Jeff asked.

Glynnis flashed a questioning glance at Laine, and Laine looked first at Jeff, then back again to the elderly woman.

"Check it out?" Jeff suggested.

Glynnis lifted the doll's dress. "Yes, she has been stitched." She glanced at Laine. "What do you think?"

Laine felt excitement rising within her.

"I say we check it out," Jeff said. "It can't hurt."

Laine nodded. "I think Jeff's right. If Kathleen told Becca that Penny was precious and she should take good care of her, I think we may have something."

She rose and crossed to Becca, kneeling at her side. "Becca, could we check inside Penny and see if your mom put something inside her? Maybe we're wrong, but no matter what, I promise to sew her back up as good as new."

Though Becca looked bewildered, she nodded her head in agreement. Within minutes, Laine loosened the stitches. She slid her fingers carefully inside the rag doll, and her heart stood still. All eyes were on her.

"What?" Jeff asked. "You found something, didn't you?"

She nodded. "Yes. Here's the answer to our question." She pulled her hand from the stuffing, bringing with it Kathleen's diamond wedding ring, an emerald necklace, and a folded piece of paper.

Glynnis gasped as the gems came into view. "My mother's emerald necklace. I'm so grateful. And the wedding ring."

Becca gazed at the jewels with curiosity. "Are these my diamonds?"

"They sure look like it, don't they, Becca?" Jeff said, standing beside her.

Laine patted her head. "This is where your mom put them for safety. When you grow up, Becca, they'll be yours to wear, but for now, we'll find a safer place for them, okay?"

Becca nodded, studying the pieces of jewelry. But the others focused on the folded paper.

With trembling hands, Laine opened it. A small key dropped to the table. In lengthy silence, she scanned the note, finally looking at the others. "I'll read it," she said.

> *This key fits a safety deposit box at the Troy Federal Bank. What I could salvage is there, except these favorite pieces that I kept at home, hoping Scott wouldn't notice the others were missing. A friend suggested I hide these, so I've put them here, praying Laine or someone who loves Becca will find them.*

An overwhelming sense of sadness washed over Laine as she struggled to control her emotions. She bit her lip and refocused on Kathleen's note. Then with tears filling her eyes, Laine turned to the child. "But, Becca, the best part is a note from your mom to you."

"To me?" Her eyes widened, her voice only a whisper.

Laine furtively wiped away the tears sneaking from her eyes. "Yes, to you. It says:

> *Becca, someday you'll be old enough to wear the lovely jewels. I wish I could be there to see you. But most of all, I hope you will listen to these words and hold them in your heart.*

Aunt Laine will help you understand.

Laine swallowed back the lump in her throat, and focusing her misty eyes, she continued to read.

> *"Do not store up for yourselves treasures on earth, where moth and rust destroy, and where thieves break in and steal. But store up for yourselves treasures in heaven. For where your treasure is, there your heart will be also."*
> *All my love forever,*
> *Mommy*

Laine looked from Jeff to Glynnis, then to Becca. Though the child seemed confused, the adults understood. Kathleen's gift to her daughter was far more precious than the diamond ring and emeralds glittering on the table.

❧

While Jeff drove Glynnis home, Laine sat next to Becca and stitched Penny back together. With the raggedy doll back in the child's arms, she tucked Becca into bed and placed the note from Kathleen on the nightstand.

Laine gazed down at Becca with Penny nestled in her arms and Bonnie curled in a ball at her side. Kissing the child good night, Laine bowed her head, praying that she could be the best aunt in the world.

She tiptoed to the doorway, watching until she saw Becca's steady, even breathing, then she closed the door and walked to the kitchen.

So much had happened in these past months. More than she could ever imagine. Today overwhelmed her. God had brought everything to a perfect ending. Every good and wonderful gift she could have asked for had been given to her. And Kathleen's final gift to Becca filled her with awe.

She returned to the porch as Jeff's footsteps sounded outside. He opened the door quietly and paused, looking at her without speaking, then sat beside her on the wicker love seat.

The last vestiges of sunset had melted into the horizon, and the full moon sprinkled the dark water with diamonds of its own, dancing and glinting on the ripples that rolled into the shore. The simple sounds of the quiet night blended into one melody: water lapping on the shore, the chirping of a cricket, and the beating of their hearts.

"You know, Jeff," Laine murmured, "I don't understand why Kathleen didn't tell me about the doll. She never mentioned that poor raggedy thing held what was left of her fortune. What a paradox. One Penny worth a fortune—in so many ways."

"I think you know the answer to that question," Jeff answered. "You said it earlier. Kathleen's treasure wasn't in the doll. Her treasure was her faith in God and Becca. . .and in you too, Laine. And I imagine she thought she had more time. . .just like you did."

He slid his arm around her, and Laine leaned her head against his shoulder.

Silence hung in the air again, then Laine turned her eyes toward Jeff. In a few months, she'd be his wife. They'd known each other such a short time, but they'd agreed: Their meeting was God's doing, God's gift. They shared the most important things life had to offer: their faith, their values, their trust, and their love.

Jeff studied Laine's pensive face and asked, "What are you thinking?"

"About you. About us, really. I'm thinking how strange

things are sometimes. How we met and how much you mean to me."

He lifted Laine's fingers and kissed them. Her diamond sparkled in the moonlight, but not nearly so brightly as the love that glowed in her eyes. She leaned forward, pressing her palm against his cheek, and lowered her lips to his, and he drank in the sweetness of her love, far better than any earthly drink.

He longed to hold her in his arms, to know her as God intended for a man to know the woman he loved, and he knew that time was near. Three months and they would be husband and wife. He smiled, feeling their entwined hands and knowing their hearts were woven together as well.

"Jeff," Laine said, leaning her head on his shoulder, "have we shared all our secrets? You have no other names, identities, worries hiding inside you? Nothing else that I should know?"

He chuckled. "Nope. I laid it all on the table. You know all my secrets. How about you?"

"Not one thing. Everything's in the open. Oh. . .well, except. . ." She paused, gazing at him.

His stomach knotted. "What?"

"I suppose you should know I don't like okra."

"Okra!"

She giggled and pulled away from him, dashing through the outer doorway into the balmy evening air.

He caught the door before it slammed and followed her, catching her by the hand. "Why did you scare me?"

"Oh, I like to see your wide eyes like the first day we met." She chuckled.

"Come here, You." He drew her into his arms and pinned her against him.

"Be kind," she teased. "Don't punish me with your kisses."

"Ah-ha, so that's what you fear."

His lips sought Laine's, and in the rippling moonlight, she clung to his embrace, giving him her lips and her heart. His intake of breath thrilled her, knowing his love was as strong and fervent as her own. Filled with completeness, she raised her eyes to the glowing, star-speckled sky and thanked God for all His precious gifts. On their wedding night, she would share with Jeff her most precious gift. No diamonds or emeralds, not one sapphire, but her pure, untarnished love.

A Letter To Our Readers

Dear Reader:

In order that we might better contribute to your reading enjoyment, we would appreciate your taking a few minutes to respond to the following questions. We welcome your comments and read each form and letter we receive. When completed, please return to the following:

Rebecca Germany, Fiction Editor
Heartsong Presents
PO Box 719
Uhrichsville, Ohio 44683

1. Did you enjoy reading *Secrets Within* by Gail Gaymer Martin?
   ❑ Very much! I would like to see more books by this author!
   ❑ Moderately. I would have enjoyed it more if

   _____

   _____

2. Are you a member of **Heartsong Presents**? Yes ❑ No ❑
   If no, where did you purchase this book?_____

   _____

3. How would you rate, on a scale from 1 (poor) to 5 (superior), the cover design?_____

4. On a scale from 1 (poor) to 10 (superior), please rate the following elements.

   _____ Heroine   _____ Plot

   _____ Hero   _____ Inspirational theme

   _____ Setting   _____ Secondary characters

5. These characters were special because _____

   _____

   _____

6. How has this book inspired your life? _____

   _____

   _____

7. What settings would you like to see covered in future
   Heartsong Presents books?_____

   _____

   _____

8. What are some inspirational themes you would like to see
   treated in future books?_____

   _____

   _____

9. Would you be interested in reading other **Heartsong
   Presents** titles?   Yes ❏   No ❏

10. Please check your age range:
    ❏ Under 18   ❏ 18-24   ❏ 25-34
    ❏ 35-45   ❏ 46-55   ❏ Over 55

Name _____

Occupation _____

Address _____

City _____ State _____ Zip _____

Email _____

Hearts♥ng

HEARTSONG PRESENTS *TITLES AVAILABLE NOW:*

(If ordering from this page, please remember to include it with the order form.)

Presents

Hearts♥ng Presents
Love Stories Are Rated G!

That's for godly, gratifying, and of course, great! If you love a thrilling love story but don't appreciate the sordidness of some popular paperback romances, **Heartsong Presents** is for you. In fact, **Heartsong Presents** is the *only inspirational romance book club* featuring love stories where Christian faith is the primary ingredient in a marriage relationship.

Sign up today to receive your first set of four never-before-published Christian romances. Send no money now; you will receive a bill with the first shipment. You may cancel at any time without obligation, and if you aren't completely satisfied with any selection, you may return the books for an immediate refund!

Imagine. . .four new romances every four weeks—two historical, two contemporary—with men and women like you who long to meet the one God has chosen as the love of their lives. . .all for the low price of $9.97 postpaid.

To join, simply complete the coupon below and mail to the address provided. **Heartsong Presents** romances are rated G for another reason: They'll arrive *Godspeed!*